Lynde Palmer

The Honorable Club

And Other Tales

Lynde Palmer

The Honorable Club
And Other Tales

ISBN/EAN: 9783337082451

Printed in Europe, USA, Canada, Australia, Japan

Cover: Foto ©Andreas Hilbeck / pixelio.de

More available books at **www.hansebooks.com**

THE

HONORABLE CLUB,

AND

OTHER TALES.

BY

LYNDE PALMER,

AUTHOR OF "THE LITTLE CAPTAIN," "HELPS OVER HARD
PLACES," ETC.

PUBLISHED BY THE

AMERICAN TRACT SOCIETY,

117 WASHINGTON STREET, BOSTON,
HURD AND HOUGHTON, 13 ASTOR PLACE, N. Y.
The Riverside Press, Cambridge, Mass.

CONTENTS.

.

THE HONORABLE CLUB.

THE HONORABLE CLUB.

CHAPTER I.

THE CODE OF THE HONORABLES.

"I DON'T believe it!" cried Paul Thornton, president of "The Honorable Club;" while a red spot burned on his smooth young cheek. "I know Miles Clavering a little too well for that. He's the best boy in the whole club. He'd cut off his right hand rather than tell a lie."

"It might make some difference, though, if he thought he would never be found out," said Jim Fuller; an ill-natured smile making his small eyes a little smaller, and his broad sullen mouth a little larger.

7

" You look like a head on an old china teapot!" cried Charley Peterson, the vice-president, impetuously.

" Do I, indeed ? " began Jim; but Paul interposed, —

"Hush, Charley! we must attend to business now. — And, Jim," said he, turning, " you must not, *shall* not, say such things about Miles, unless you can prove every word you say ; unless you —"

" Well, I can," interrupted Jim. " It was one day last February, a cold, snowy day. I remember it just as well; and brother Ben and I —"

"Never mind," said Paul, a little impatiently ; " you've told it all once. The best way of settling it will be to have a trial; and, when all the members are together, we will hear your story and his story, and judge between you."

" Oh, yes! that's the best way. The club has never had a trial before ! " cried

Charley eagerly, and then blushed to think he had forgotten in his excitement what a mortification it would be to Miles.

"Yes, that will be the best way," echoed Jim Fuller, with the same ill-natured smile; "and then, perhaps, you will see who has the best right to be a member of the club, and whether you didn't make a mistake when you blackballed me."

"Ah, I see now!" cried fiery Charley. "You're just as jealous as you can be; and you're just getting that up to be revenged on Miles, because —"

"You'll see more one of these days," cried Jim, angrily. "How soon will the trial be?"

"Next Saturday," said Paul, with a sigh: "the sooner the better."

"And where shall we meet?" continued Jim.

"You needn't say *we*," muttered Charley; but, fortunately, Jim didn't hear.

"At our barn," said Paul, considering. "There's a nice room over the stables, where we boys have kept our tools. I'll clear it up, and have the court sit there."

"Very well," said Jim; "and I can tell you —"

"Good-morning, Jim," interrupted Paul, with little ceremony. "I haven't looked at my Latin yet;" and he walked rapidly away, accompanied by Charley.

"The Honorable Club" to which the boys made such frequent allusion had been in existence about a year. The idea had been first suggested by Paul's Uncle Harry, and had met with immense favor from the moment the plan was unfolded. It was to be a club for the promotion of everything that was noble and honorable; and no boy could belong to it without being willing to sign his name to sundry articles of agreement, among which the following were the most important : —

"We, the undersigned, promise, —

" 1. Always to speak the truth.

" 2. To be strictly honest " (and this rule extended even to those small lines of trade, — swapping marbles and pocket-knives).

" 3. To be charitable to the faults of others; and never to speak evil of another, especially behind his back.

" 4. To be generous in giving to the poor, and in helping them, now and then, with strong young hands.

" 5. To be courteous and polite; very respectful to the aged; attentive to the mothers and sisters; obliging to all, — even to the giving of cold water to the little ones.

" 6. In honor to prefer one another.

" 7. To ask daily for God's help to keep all these promises."

A little codicil at the end provided, that, in case of any flagrant violation of these rules, the offending member should be tried by a jury of their own number, and acquitted, or sentenced according to the magnitude of his offense.

There was also provision made for the admission of new members. A "business-meeting" was held at such important seasons. A table was set before the president, upon which was a box, and a liberal supply of black and white buttons. The members then approached in single file: each made choice of a button, and dropped it into the box. When the voting was over, the president examined the box. If the buttons were all white, the candidate was accepted; but, alas! if *black*, he had to retire in great mortification.

Now, it happened, a little more than six months before, that Miles Clavering and James Fuller moved into Barrytown the very same week. They had not been long in the village before they found out that

the young "Honorables," as everybody
called them, were greatly esteemed, and
that kind Uncle Harry was continually
planning some pleasant surprise for them.
Sometimes it was a nutting expedition, or
an excursion to the city; or, as winter
came on, tea-parties in his nice old-bachelor
home, with stories and games in the evening.

Miles and James soon were eagerly re-
questing admission, and the Honorables
met to debate thereon. Every one had
something good to say of Miles,—"generous, polite, warm-hearted;" the white buttons almost jumped into the hat of themselves, and Miles was admitted with cheers.

Then came Jim's turn. There was an
ominous hesitation, then a whisper, among
the Honorables, — "selfish, discontented,
sullen." The members filed slowly past.
As the last dropped his button, Charley
stretched his neck over the president's

shoulder, and peered into the box. "Black
as a crow!" cried he. "I declare, not a
white feather among 'em!"

So Jim was rejected, to his bitter indignation. To live in Barrytown, and not be
one of the Honorables; not to have one
of those wonderful blue badges, made by
Paul's pretty sister, with the letters "H. C.,"
in the brightest gold-thread, curiously
wrought thereon, — it was almost unbeara-
ble: it was ignominy to one of Jim's passionate nature.

Poor, unhappy, sullen Jim! He certainly
deserved some pity; but the young "Honorables" didn't at all realize his misery. If
they had only given him some encouragement, some hope that, by good conduct, he
might some day apply again, and snap his
fingers at the black buttons! But no: they
all passed him by, and went home very
complacently. It was so comfortable to
have the little world at Barrytown see that

they were possessed of certain virtues which every boy, Jim Fuller for instance, didn't have! They never suspected this little serpent of vanity, so cunningly coiled up in their really brave young hearts.

As for Jim, he went his way with face more sullen than ever.

"If *I* can not wear the blue badge," said he bitterly to himself, "I mean to have company. Miles shall not crow over me long."

And from that hour Jim was watching, with patience worthy of a better cause, that he might catch his rival slipping. At last the longed-for opportunity came. Miles's young feet were led into temptation. Did they find the way to escape? Jim thinks not; and we shall find out at the trial.

CHAPTER II.

OW, where was Miles this same pleasant summer day, while friends and
enemies were so busy with his name?
If, when school was out, you had gone
down that quiet lane, and stood under the
great elm by Miss Pringle's cottage-garden,
you would have heard in about five minutes a cheery whistle, and a pair of boots
keeping lively time thereto. In a moment
more, the company marching to this im-
promptu fife and drum would have come in
sight, — a pair of the merriest blue eyes,
ditto of bronzed crimson cheeks, and a large
frank mouth, now a little out of its original

16

shape, being screwed up for the aforementioned musical purposes till it looked like a capital O, just as if it were a kind of an exclamation beginning a sentence which the rest of the merry face finished, — "Oh," what a pleasant world! "Oh," what a happy life!

The busy feet stopped at Miss Pringle's gate. Miss Pringle was getting old. The rheumatism had stiffened her up cruelly the past winter, and she didn't seem to get thawed out yet. Poor old soul! it took her almost half an hour to get down on her knees to weed a bed in her garden, and nobody knew how long she was in getting up again. Miles had happened to see this performance one morning a few days ago. Some boys would have thought it great fun; but the Honorables did not laugh at such things; Uncle Harry had taught them better. No! instead of this, he jumped right over the fence, gave her his strong young arm, and helped her carefully upon her feet again.

" Why don't you have a gardener, Miss Pringle ? " he cried.

" Why, child," said the panting old lady, " I did have one one day this spring; but he charged me so much I couldn't buy any meat for a fortnight; so I am obliged to do the work myself."

Miles knew she was very poor, and yet that she couldn't bear to give up her pretty garden, with its gay borders. She took such a pride in it! It was almost the only comfort the poor old lady had.

Something made Miles very uneasy. He couldn't get away, although it was Saturday, and the boys were going to have a game of ball upon the green.

" How much I could do for her in an hour! " he thought. Still, Miles didn't like work any better than other boys. Then he hesitated a little more, and looked at his blue badge, with its letters blazing in the sun.

"Pshaw!" said he to himself; "I've no right to call myself an Honorable if I can't make that little sacrifice;" and hurriedly, for fear he should repent, he offered his services to Miss Pringle.

The old lady couldn't believe her ears, so she thought she would try her eyes. She wiped her spectacles, and put them on again, and then looked hard into the pleasant, frank face. Gradually, as she looked, her poor, thin lips began to quiver. It was only a smile coming; but, as it did not come very often, it took so long to settle itself that it was some time before Miles could guess what was the matter with her mouth. At last it was a real, unmistakable look of pleasure.

"You are good and honest, my dear," said the old lady, heartily. "I know those blue eyes. But it seems very strange that

a young, active boy like you should be willing to leave his play and work for an old
woman. Thank you most kindly, my dear!
May the Lord bless you ' "

And Miles, feeling very warm all over,
but very happy withal, did a wonderful
amount of work in an hour, to Miss Pringle's great admiration and satisfaction.

" I didn't know there were any such boys
left," said the old lady, at the end.

" Oh, but I belong to the Honorables!"
cried Miles, pointing a little proudly to his
blue badge. "Any of our boys would do
the same thing." And away he went over
the fence, — he never could stop for a gate,
— his mouth curled into the capital " O ; "
and he and his whistle were out of the lane
before Miss Pringle could turn round.

" He won't come back again," she thought,
as a day or two passed without him. But
here, this pleasant June afternoon, school
just out, and plenty of fun going on, —

here was her faithful young gardener again. The tears came into poor Miss Pringle's eyes,—she hardly knew why,—and she brought her camp-stool and knitting out to a dry spot: it was so pleasant to be near that fresh young face, and to hear him whistle at his work!

"Did you ever see such handsome tulips anywhere?" said Miss Pringle, at last, as he stopped and wiped his forehead.

"I don't think I ever did," said Miles, good-naturedly.

"You don't know how I like to see 'em holding up their red and yellow cups, so as if they wanted the Lord to use 'em for something," continued the old lady.

"They do make a very pretty set of goblets, that's a fact," laughed Miles. "If the fairies should want to give a dinner-party now!"

But the old lady was thinking, and didn't seem to hear. "Yes: I love to see 'em

there, so free from weeds," she said, presently. "And the lilies and the violets,
too, — how sweet they are! I think the
Lord loves us, my dear, for helping his flowers along, and giving them a chance to
grow so grand and sweet. Besides pleasing
an old woman, I think you have been doing
something for the Lord this afternoon."

"I don't think I understand you, ma'am,"
said Miles, very politely, while his thoughts
were far away, wondering whether the boys
were playing ball or going in swimming.

"It's just my notion," said the old lady,
smiling; "but, some way, I want to tell
you about it. Now, suppose you were far
away from home, and should want to send
something to your little brother; and suppose you should make him, say, a little ship,
with cunning little ropes and spars, and
should paint it very fine, thinking all the
time, 'How pleased Georgie will be when
he gets it! he will think it so beautiful! he

will wonder how I could ever think of such clever things.' Then suppose that the person who was taking your ship home should be careless, and should let the spars get broken, and the little cord ropes get all in a tangle, and knock off the paint, so that Georgie would hardly look at the old thing."

" That would be downright mean," cried Miles, a little interested.

" Wait a bit," said the old lady. " Then suppose your friend Paul got hold of it, painted it, and fitted it all up again, and said to Georgie, ' This is the present Miles meant to send you.' What would you think of Paul ?"

" I'd say that was just like a good, warm friend ; and I'd love him for it."

" Right," said the old lady, with a pleased face. " Now, don't you know that the Lord made everything very good, and flowers among the rest, so fair and sweet, that we can hardly guess how wonderful they were?

Then sin came, and weeds; and men were
careless, and they let the poor things get
choked and dwindle away. Now, *I* think,"
said the old lady vehemently, "that when
any one loves a flower, and keeps all the
weeds away, and puts it in a nice, generous
soil, and gives it water, and takes care of
it—like a baby you may say—till it grows
just as grand as it can be,—like those pansies there, maybe, with their great purple-
velvet leaves,—*I* believe the Lord is pleased.
It seems like honoring him, you know, and
saying to everybody, 'See! this is what the
Lord meant when he first thought of a vio-
let.'" The old lady laughed softly to herself. "That's just my notion, though; and
I never spoke to the minister about it: but
I just can't help believing that the Lord is
pleased when we find out his beautiful
thoughts."

"Well, now, that *is* curious," said Miles;
but, as he looked around the fair little gar-

den glowing in the sunset, he added, "I
don't know why it shouldn't be so, either;"
and obeying a sudden impulse, at which he
laughed himself, he took off his hat, and
made a low bow to the pansies.

"What are you thinking of now?" said
Miss Pringle, as she caught Miles's merry
eyes fixed on her face. "Am I the queerest old woman you ever saw? What do I
look like? Come, now?"

"Just like one of your old brown roots,"
thought Miles, casting an involuntary glance
at a heap of bulbs at his feet.

"Like that old withered root, eh?" said
the old lady, a little sharply.

"I didn't say so," stammered Miles.

"Your eyes speak just as plain as your
tongue, child; but I'm not angry," said she,
a little more mildly. "Only remember,
my dear, that the good Lord made the old
root, and you can't tell what may spring
from it yet. Some day, when I've been
transplanted to the heavenly gardens, I ex-

pect to be beautiful. 'It is sown a natural body, it is raised a spiritual body,'" added the old lady, softly, to herself.

"Beautiful!" echoed innocent, outspoken Miles; "and how will I know you then?"

The old lady laughed good-naturedly. "You know the pretty scarlet and yellow tulips when they grow out of their old roots, and the sweet white lilies when they come up so pure out of their brown little bulbs: so, when you see me, you'll know me in a minute. You'll say, 'That flower could only have grown out of the old Pringle root.'"

Miles's look of comical perplexity made the old lady laugh again; and she was just beginning to enlarge upon the subject, when a voice called, —

"Miles, Miles! Oh, here you are!" and six or eight young Honorables suddenly appeared at the fence.

"Just ready," said Miles, hurrying on his coat.

CHAPTER III.

"HAT'S going on?" asked Miles, cheerily, as they walked rapidly down the lane. "Uncle Harry isn't getting up his strawberry party already, is he?"

"No," said Dick Wharton. "Charley said he was going to find you, and we just came along for the walk."

"Oh, that's all!" said Miles. "What have you all been doing since school was out?"

"I've been working for father," said Dick, "to earn money for the Fourth of July."

"How much do you think I've earned

27

this spring?" cried Miles. "Almost twenty shillings! The next time mother goes to the city she is going to buy me the best kind of books;—a history of the French Revolution,—they say you could sit up all night to read it,—and some wonderful books of travels. I'll lend them all to the club when I get them."

"That will be capital," said Dick.

"And I've worked real hard for them, too," said Miles, rubbing his hands. "That makes it so much the better. How happy I do feel this summer!" rattled on the boy. "Do you know I can't help feeling sorry for Jim sometimes? It must be a dreadful trial not to belong to our club. Why, I'm so proud of it— What's the matter, Charley?" cried he suddenly, catching Charley's eyes fixed on him with a troubled expression.

"Yes, Charley has hardly opened his

mouth for an hour," said Dick. "What's the trouble, old fellow?"

"I have been feeling a little vexed," said Charley. "Some one has been accusing one of our members of doing something very wrong."

The boys looked in some consternation from one to another, and a half dozen tender consciences hung out a red banner of alarm in as many pairs of cheeks.

"You don't mean me, Charley?" "It isn't I, is it?" resounded on every side, for these young Honorables had the rare grace of suspecting themselves before others.

"No, no," said Charley; but Miles in his astonishment had not asked the question.

"I am sent by the president," proceeded Charley, slowly, "to tell that boy he is under arrest, and must give bail to attend his trial next Saturday morning at nine o'clock."

There was a profound silence. Charley

turned towards Miles, colored violently, then looked down, saying, with a forced laugh, "Pshaw! it's only a kind of a joke, but some way it seems so real I can't do it."

The merry blue eyes were clouded. "You can't mean me, Charley?" said Miles, huskily.

Charley did not speak.

"Not Miles!" cried a chorus of voices, expressing every shade of surprise, indignation, and grief.

"Don't mind it, Charley," said Miles, bravely, in a minute; "I surrender; I'm your prisoner."

"Who accuses him?" cried Dick, furiously.

"Jim Fuller," said Charley. "He insists that he has broken the first article. Of course I don't believe it, but according to our agreement he'll have to be tried, you know. Of course he'll come out triumphant."

"Not a doubt of that," cried Dick, echoed by the chorus. "You're not afraid, are you, Miles?"

"No," said he, slowly. "I know what Jim means, but I think I can make it all right."

"Hurrah!" cried Dick. "Miles, you must let me be your lawyer; I'll reason you out of everything. You don't know how clever I am. I'm getting as conceited as that old fellow who thought he was the key to every lock in creation."

Miles laughed, and grasped his hand.

"And I'll go bail;" "and I;" "and I;" cried more eager friends. "What is the bail, Charley?"

"Four jack-knives," laughed Charley; and they were speedily handed out.

"Now let's go and have a game of ball, or something. Come, Miles."

"Not to-night," said Miles, pleasantly, waving them off. "I must go home and

3

prepare for my lawyer. · Dick, you will come and see me in the evening?"

"Never fail," cried Dick.

Miles walked away bravely enough, but as soon as he had turned the corner his head dropped, and a great round tear fell plump upon the pretty blue badge. "I have been so proud of it," said he, patting it tenderly. "What shall I do if the boys say I haven't any right to wear it?"

CHAPTER IV.

ANOTHER June day, fresh and fair, with boundless blue sky at its head, and sweet, dewy grass at its feet.

Miles had been up since four o'clock, for it was Saturday, *the* Saturday, the most momentous day of his life, Miles thought. Five long hours before the trial.

He tried to study, and thought he was studying, for half an hour; then he had to look at the back of his book, to see whether he had his algebra or grammar. Then Georgie's shrill voice attracted him to the garden: "Who'll mend my horse? The wheel is off." Miles tried, and broke the poor animal all to pieces.

3   33

"Don't cry, Georgie; I'll buy you a new one to-morrow, but I'm in such a hurry now;" and off he walked at the greatest speed a few steps, and then stopped short to think what on earth he had started to do.

Then the breakfast bell rang. Miles couldn't eat. "What is the matter?" cried sister Minnie.

"He don't hear you," said Georgie, as Miles sat with his eyes fixed on the chandelier; "he hasn't minded a word I've said this morning."

"Miles," said mischievous Minnie, suddenly, "come in. What makes you stand out there in the rain, and bare-headed too?"

Miles started, clapped his hands to his head, looked in a bewildered way at the ceiling, and finally came to himself, amid peals of laughter from the whole family.

In the mean time there was a great commotion in Mr. Thornton's barn. The loft had been carefully swept, benches had been hastily constructed for the jury and the public, and one or two kitchen chairs had been impressed to accommodate the judge and the lawyers.

There was some trouble in getting up the jury. After taking out the judge and lawyers, Miles and his guard, there were only eleven members left, and it was felt to be highly illegal to conduct proceedings with less than twelve jurors.

Charley Peterson at last rather timidly proposed making up the deficiency with a girl.

"That would do," said Dick. "There's Jenny Seabright; she's very dignified, and would look well upon the bench."

But Charley Peterson made a mysterious communication, to the effect that this young lady had just bought some new hoops, and probably wouldn't give the least attention to the trial, no matter how important it was.

for it took her whole mind to think how she should get through doors. Besides, the accommodations were limited, and he was quite sure, if she came, half of the jurors would have to sit on the floor. "Now I propose," concluded Charley, "little Mabel Thornton, the judge's sister; small, but of good sense, and no more skirts than a hearth-brush."

Charley's motion was seconded with applause, and the small juror was picked up in the back yard, pink sun-bonnet and all, and conveyed to her responsible post, with admonitions to look as wise as possible, and only stir when she couldn't possibly help it.

Now everything was complete, and Paul took his seat behind the table, covered with his mother's old shawl.

"Steady, boys; sit light!" cried Charley to the jurors, as the old bench creaked ominously.

"Silence!" cried Paul, and rang his big

bell for the guard to bring in the prisoner.

At sight of the pleasant blue eyes, the little court, entirely out of order, burst into a storm of applause.

Jim Fuller, coming in, heard it with a bitter heart. "That's just the way of the world," said the young cynic to himself. "I never told a lie in my life, but no one thinks of giving me a pleasant word. I am not thought fit to associate with the Honorables;" and he glanced contemptuously at Miles.

Alas, poor Jim! Could he not see that there were other articles of the honorable code which he had never thought of keeping, and that this truth upon which he prided himself was often so unnecessarily told, with such mean motives behind it, that it only made him more unlovable than ever?

But to return to the trial. The room

was quite rapidly filling up with sisters and cousins, who, in some way, had got wind of the matter; even Jenny Seabright, hoops and all, had managed to squeeze in, and was talking volubly to her next neighbor.

"I'll never believe that dear Miles could do anything mean. Why, one day, in a pouring rain, he carried our little Susy all the way —" But the bell rang again, and you might have heard a pin drop.

Then Jim arose with some embarrassment, for every one in the house looked frowningly upon him, with the sole exception of faithful little brother Bennie, whom he held tightly by the hand.

"It all happened last February," began Jim, doggedly, "the very last of the month. It was cold and snowy, and Ben and I were walking down the street. As we were passing old Rinkel's store, Ben saw a great pyramid of figs and oranges in the window, and *would* stop to look at them. Just then

Jack, the store boy, looked out, and asked me if I wouldn't come in and stay a minute, while he ran somewhere, I couldn't make out for what. I told him no, for I was in a great hurry; and, besides, I didn't think it was right for him to leave the store when old Rinkel was away. He began to abuse me, and call me disobliging, and other hard names. That's all the reward I ever get for trying to do right."

" Humph ! " said Charley.

" Stick to the point," cried Paul.

" Well," continued Jim, in an aggrieved tone, " just then Miles came strolling along, and Jack asked him. Of course Miles said ' yes,' because it was easier; he never has the courage to say ' no.' "

" That has nothing to do with your story," cried Paul, impatiently.

Jim scowled. " I'm telling it as fast as I can.— Then Miles went in; they had some talk, and Jack flew out the back door.

Pretty soon back he came with — what do you think? — a shovelful of live coals! I thought I'd better look into the matter a little, and went into the store."

"I thought you were in a hurry," interposed Charley; and a titter ran along the jury.

The judge rapped, and Jim continued: "Jack was whispering again to Miles as I came in, and I just caught a few words: 'Through the barn, — shortest cut, — and I stumbled, — spilled half my coals.'

"Miles looked a little frightened.

"'Don't be uneasy,' said Jack. 'I got them up safe again, every one, though I burned my whole ten fingers. I looked sharp, I can tell you.'

"All very well," continued Jim, telling his story with infinite relish; "but whose barn was on fire just half an hour after?"

"How should *we* know?" growled Charley.

" You remember well enough," retorted Jim. " I hurried right back with Benny at the first alarm, and there was Miles working away like mad. He knew well enough who was to blame, but he couldn't work hard enough to wipe out that mistake. I was glad I'd had sense enough to keep out of the scrape.

" Old Rinkel arrived just as the barn burned clean down to the ground, and oh! how he did storm! He said he knew it was set on fire, and he'd find out who did it. Whoever did it should spend his summer in jail, if there was any law in the land. There stood Jack, pale as a ghost, leaning up against a barrel, and Miles was in the door, looking pretty white too. Now, thinks I, Miles will tell the whole truth, especially as he is a member of the Honorable Club. But no, not a word. Instead of that, — would you believe it? — he actually let old Rinkel praise him up! ' There's a brave, honest boy,' said the old fellow; ' they tell me he worked like a young tiger, and got my horse out safe too. There's many a man wouldn't have had the pluck and good sense ; ' and old Rinkel, who is tight as the bark of a tree, actually gave Miles a cracker and a tumbler of cider, and ordered me to get up and give him my chair. I thought some day he would find out what a mistake he was making."

" How everybody loves him ! " whispered Jenny Seabright, while the small juror was preparing to get down and kiss the prisoner, to Charley's pretended horror, who with great difficulty recalled her to the dignities of her position.

Jim was not at all pleased with the impression he was making. " I haven't come to the worst yet," said he, hurriedly, while Miles bit his lip. " Old Rinkel went out to mourn over his barn again, and Jack, creeping up to Miles, began whispering; I

couldn't hear what he said, but I suppose
he was promising Miles something if he'd
only keep dark."

"You've no right to suppose anything
about it," cried Dick. "Tell the bare facts,
and get done."

Jim swallowed his indignation, and went
on. "Pretty soon old Rinkel was back,
storming harder than ever, saying he had
lost a great deal, — he didn't believe the
insurance would half cover it, and he meant
to find out who played him this mean trick.
Then he asked Jack if there was any one
hanging around the barn while he was
gone.

"'No, sir,' said Jack.

"'You were right here all the time?'

"'Yes, sir,' said he.

"'Was anybody in the store while I was
gone?'

"'The Doctor, and Mrs. Carey's girl,
and Miles; that's all,' said Jack.

"' How long were you here, Miles?' said old Rinkel.

"' About a quarter of an hour,' said he.

"' You didn't see anything out of the way, did you?'

" Miles gave a little faint answer. ' Hey?' said old Rinkel, turning sharp around; '*you* haven't the least notion how it happened, have you?'

" Jack gave a little cough, and turned whiter than chalk, and Miles looked square into old Rinkel's face, and said,—

"' No, sir.'

" That's all I've got to say," said Jim, sitting down, and wiping his red face.

There was consternation in the little court for a minute. The jurors looked at Paul, and Paul looked at the ceiling; Miles turned red and white twenty times in a minute. The small juror's white apron quivered with a deep, deep sigh, and half the company were just ready to cry, it seemed so serious, when there was a sudden crash and shriek, and the jurors' bench and the dignity of the court all came to grief together. Jenny Seabright almost went into hysterics to see the bewildered pink sunbonnet emerging from such a tangle of arms and legs. In fact, every one had a hearty laugh, and felt better after it.

" That monkey of a Charley Peterson did it on purpose," muttered Jim ; but nobody seemed to hear, and as soon as order was restored, Paul motioned to lawyer Dick to open the case for his client.

" Boys," began the vehement Dick, —" I beg your pardon, your *honor*, and gentlemen of the jury,—I beg to state the true circumstances under which my honorable friend was brought into this unpleasant position. I will not deny that my client was walking down street that February day, just as Mr. James Fuller, being pressed for time, and oppressed with a sense of duty, had re-

fused to oblige Jack Carter. So far Mr.
Fuller is perfectly correct; but it might interest the court to know the reasons Jack
(who is a faithful boy) gave for wishing to
leave the store. The fire had gone out in
the stove, — Jack had forgotten to shake it
down or something, — and it was quite a ca-
lamity. Old Rinkel was such a close man,
he only let Jack have just so much kindling
in the morning, and the rest he locked up.
He'd been trying most an hour with bits of
paper to start it up again, but it wouldn't
go, and old Rinkel would scold terribly
when he came back all chilly and found
no fire to warm himself; so he begged
'wouldn't one of the boys just keep store
while he ran through the alley to his mother's and got a few light-sticks?' Of course
my kind-hearted client stayed for shaky,
little, nervous Jack.

"Pretty soon, sure enough, back comes
Jack with a shovelful of hot coals. Miles

was frightened. ' How could your mother
let you do so ? ' said he.

" ' She wasn't in the kitchen,' said Jack,
' and the coals looked so nice, as if they'd
start the fire in half a minute, I just took a
shovelful and ran. Now, if I can only get
the fire nicely going before he comes, *won't*
I be a lucky dog ? '

" ' But, Jack,' said Miles, still looking
alarmed, ' I hope you didn't bring them
through the barn ? '

" ' I had to,' said Jack ; ' there's no other
door to the alley.'

" ' Were you very careful ? '

" ' I guess you would have thought so,'
said Jack, ' for, to tell the truth, I stumbled, and spilt one or two, and I stayed and
hunted till there wasn't a spark left as big
as a fire-fly.'

" ' I think I'd better go out and look at
the barn,' said Miles.

" ' Nonsense ! ' said Jack ; ' you couldn't

look sharper than I did;' and Miles went home.

"About half an hour afterwards, as Jim says, the barn was burned to the ground.

"Miles was there the first one. He went right into the smoke and blaze, wrapped his coat around old Dolly's head, and led her out. Then he worked away at the engine as hard as any grown man, and *I* say he deserved every bit of praise old Rinkel gave him."

An approving murmur ran along the back seats.

"As for what Mr. Fuller said afterwards, urged on by his sense of duty, I suppose," continued Dick, intending to be very sarcastic, "I have only to say, that when Jack stole up to Miles in the store there, the mysterious words that the plaintiff's long ears didn't catch were these : —

"'Don't tell it, Miles! Don't tell it, *dear* Miles. We are *so* poor, and mother is half blind. Oh, if he *should* turn me out! but that is not the worst,—I shall be sent to jail! Oh, Miles, it will kill mother, and me too!'

"The rest is very much as Mr. Fuller told it. Miles did say, 'No, sir!' but I contend that it wasn't a lie. Hadn't Jack picked up every speck of coal; and how could Miles know that the barn hadn't taken fire in some other way? He hadn't the least notion how it happened, of course, and he said so."

"That's it!" cried one or two jurors, looking much relieved. "I knew it was a mistake."

"Wait a minute," said Miles, hurriedly. "I am much obliged to Dick, but he has forgotten something I told him. I felt so uneasy about the barn that I came back before there was any alarm, and thought I saw smoke coming out of the door. So I rushed in, and there was fire coming right

up from the middle of the floor. I don't
suppose any one would have chosen such a
place to set it on fire—"

"Hush!" whispered Dick; "that's illegal. You needn't condemn *yourself:* why
don't you leave it to me?"

"No," said Miles, firmly, though there
was a mist over the blue eyes; "I'm afraid
I know very well how it happened."

The friendly jurors and sympathizing
public looked blank.

"Why won't he let himself be cleared?"
whispered Jenny. "What a dear goose he
is!" and then some one, with no sense of
propriety, cried, "Three cheers for Miles!"
and that outrageous little court nearly
brought the roof down.

"The *Honorables* are applauding a lie,"
said Jim Fuller, grimly.

"Not at all," cried Charley. "Can't
you see—"

"The case isn't finished," said Paul,

rapping. " We will examine witnesses, if
there are any."

" Will any one be angry if I move a little, Charley ? " interposed the small juror,
who hadn't dared to stir for a whole hour.
The request nearly upset the gravity of the
court again, and poor little Pink Sunbonnet
was appointed a special committee to find
out exactly what time it was by the hall
clock.

Back again with exceeding promptitude
panted the little messenger to announce
that it was " half-past ten by the hall clock,
which was slow, and a quarter of eleven by
the parlor clock, which was fast, and grand-
mother thought that just the right time
might be twenty-one minutes and twenty
seconds of eleven."

Another burst of laughter rather grieved
the innocent little heart, but Charley handed
her gallantly to her seat, whispering that
he had heard " truth lay at the bottom of

a well, but he should always know after this that she wore a white apron and pink sunbonnet."

Then followed a short examination of witnesses. The prosecution only brought forward Benny, who repeated everything Jim had told like a parrot, and said he had heard Miles tell the lie.

"Are you sure you know what the truth is?" said Charley, impatiently.

"Yes, he does," answered Jim. "He can tell you some too. What did you hear that day you went to play with Phil Peterson, Benny?"

"I heard Mrs. Peterson talking to Charley, because he'd eaten all the gingerbread, and hadn't left a bit for Susy or Phil. She said, 'Oh, Charley, that's sel—'"

"Shame, Jim! Shame, Benny!" cried several voices.

"I don't deny it," said Charley, crimson to his hair. "I was mean that day."

"Don't he say it's true himself?" asked Jim, sullenly.

"Yes," said Paul, "I suppose it was the truth, but it wasn't at all necessary to tell it. Indeed, I think nothing can be meaner than to tell anything to injure another boy's character."

An approving murmur rose from the jury.

"Then it would have been mean for Miles to have told the truth and injured Jack," retorted Jim.

"I don't say Miles ought to have told about Jack," cried Paul, "but he was asked a direct question, and should have answered truly for himself. *Your* case is very different, can't you see? Nobody asked you or Benny about Charley's selfishness. It would have been a great deal nobler, and no lie at all, if you had kept that to yourself. Uncle Harry says it is only when a *square* question knocks at the door

that you must either send the truth or a lie
to open it."

"Or else refuse to open it at all," said
Uncle Harry, who had stolen in unperceived.
"It is quite right to keep the door shut
sometimes, when, for instance, a very impertinent question knocks. I haven't much
patience with such visitors, and generally
pretend not to hear them. Silence isn't
always untruth by any means. But what's
going on here this morning?"

The case was rapidly unfolded to Uncle
Harry, who looked a little grave.

"Don't say we oughtn't to let him off,"
whispered Dick: "just hear my witnesses;"
and one after another was marched up to
prove what was already well known before,
that Miles was the kindest-hearted, politest,
best boy in town.

Sister Minnie, who had arrived breathless
about five minutes before, gave testimony
to his unselfishness at home. Friend after

friend had something to tell of his courtesy,
patience, generosity to the poor; in short,
the indefatigable Dick proved him the
brightest ornament of the club, in spite of
poor Miles's protestations and burning
cheeks. " I have also communicated with
Miss Pringle," said Dick, " who regrets that
she can not be with us, but sends her testimony to our client's character — "

" Don't, Dick," pleaded poor Miles.

But Dick remorselessly unfolded the bit
of paper and read: " The best boy I have
ever known since I laid my dear young
brother in the grave more than fifty years
ago."

Minnie and Jenny wiped their eyes.

" There !" said Dick triumphantly, " the
best boy of the last half century ! I think I
have proved that he has a better right to be
an Honorable than any of us. Let him
that is without sin cast the first stone,"
concluded he magnificently.

" Have you proved he didn't tell a lie?"
said Jim, coming in like a wet blanket.

" If he did make a little mistake just
once," cried Dick warmly, "I think it ought
to be overlooked. All the boys who read
their Bibles know that the very best of men
— Jacob and King David and Peter, all —
well, made a *mistake*, when they were
brought into temptation, and yet the Lord
seemed to specially love and honor them."

" Hold, my boy!" cried Uncle Harry.
" Not quite so fast. The Lord loved and
honored them for other virtues, but those
little ' mistakes,' as you call them, were
great sins, and had a severe punishment.
Jacob deceived his father, and by and by
his sons deceived *him*, and sold his favorite
son Joseph away from him. In fact, he had
so many troubles that in looking back upon
his life he could only say his days had been
' few and *evil*.'

" As for David, what sorrow he must have

felt when he prayed in vain for the dear little boy dying on his mother's knees, or when God took from him his beautiful grown-up son Absalom! Besides, don't you remember, the Lord wouldn't let him have the honor of building the temple? What a disappointment that must have been! Then who would have been in Peter's place when the grieved Saviour turned and looked on him! just *looked*, that was all, as if he could not believe his friend could so dishonor him. That look almost broke Peter's heart; he went out and wept bitterly. Was it a little 'mistake,' do you think, boys?"

"No! no!" cried the young jurors, looking very sober, while the red drifted out of Miles's cheeks.

Dick rallied in a minute. "But it's right sometimes to tell a lie, Uncle Harry" (all the club called him Uncle Harry); "I heard father say so once."

"When was that, Dick?" said Uncle Harry, smiling.

"Why, that day when crazy Joe came into Mrs. Simmons's house with a gun, and told her she was too good to live in this world, and he was going to send her to a better one. She was all alone in the farmhouse, and he'd just driven her into a corner, when her brother happened to come back from the field. 'That's just as you say, Joe,' said he; 'she'd better go: but let me take that gun a minute; your lock isn't just right. I'll fix it for you.'

"So Joe handed it over, as innocent as a baby, and Mr. Brown just fired it out of the window, and then caught Joe and tied him up with the clothes-line. Now suppose he hadn't cheated him, but just tried to snatch the gun, Joe would have killed Mrs. Simmons before he was half across the room. Would that have been better?"

"Very well done, Dick," said Uncle

Harry. "I suppose you think you have caught me now. Of course it was right and very clever in Mr. Brown to say what he did. But this is one of the exceptions, a peculiar case. You can not reason with a crazy man, and it is certainly right to use any means in your power to prevent him from committing a crime."

"Then, again," said Dick, a little flushed with his triumph, "let's suppose another case. Suppose there was a sort of King Herod, who sent out to kill all the little girls six years of age. Then suppose you had Mabel hid away under the bed, and men should come and say, 'Is there a little girl here? we've come to kill her!" wouldn't you say, 'No! there's no such girl here'?"

Dire dismay looked out of poor little Mabel's wide blue eyes at such a supposition.

"Never mind," whispered Charley; "they shall never get up to *your* room. I'll trip them up on the stairs."

"That's a very terrible case, Dick," laughed Uncle Harry, "and I'm rather afraid I *should* dodge a little. Time enough, though, when I find myself in such a tight spot. You know with every temptation the Lord has provided a way of escape, and I should look around for a chink somewhere. These, however, are most unusual cases, and don't come under general rules. But I'll tell you something to guide you a little, boys: in every temptation try to think what Christ would do in your place. Anything that would be wrong for him would be wrong for you."

Miles sighed heavily, and the boys looked irresolutely at one another.

"As for Miles's case," said Uncle Harry, kindly, "I can not see that it comes under any of these exceptions. I love him as much as any of you," continued he, in answer to an appealing look from Dick, "but for that very reason I want this young jury

to be very careful now. Some one has said
that all the first appearances of poisonous
plants are the same as healthy ones, and we
must look out for them. I don't want any
false ideas to take root in these fresh young
hearts. For instance, my dear boys, never
let this belief grow, that the strongest temptation or kindest of motives can make a lie
right.

"If a *boy* hasn't the courage to tell the
truth, he will grow up a man whom nobody
respects or depends upon. A lie is fatal to
true manliness; as some one has said, ' a
lie is like a worm-track in a stick of timber,
—it makes it weak and unsound.'

" As for Miles, he had great temptation.
It was a very disagreeable position. I know
he looked everywhere for escape, and then
—oh, what a pity!—jumped into a lie,—
from the frying-pan into the fire."

" Oh, Uncle Harry!" cried Miles, who
couldn't keep still any longer; "it wasn't

because I was afraid for myself at all. I'd have told the whole truth in a minute; but if you had only heard Jack—" and there was something very like a sob smothered in a sudden fit of coughing.

A sympathetic murmur arose from the tender-hearted public.

"I know it, my boy; I believe you," said Uncle Harry; "but it was a mistake nevertheless. How would it have done, do you think, if you had encouraged Jack to tell the whole story and throw himself on Mr. Rinkel's mercy? The old gentleman would have stormed a little, I haven't a doubt, but I think he would have known how to value a boy who had courage to tell the truth. I'm pretty sure he would have kept him after all, and had more confidence in him than ever. At least, you and Jack would have been a great deal happier. I think the experiment was worth trying, don't you?"

"Yes," said Miles, regretfully. "Jack
has told me he was unhappy about it a great
many times, but we didn't know exactly
what to do. Besides, Mr. Rinkel likes the
new barn he is building so much better that
he told Jack he was glad the old one had
burned down, and then we felt a great deal
better about it. It didn't seem so wrong,
but I suppose our fault was just the same;"
and poor Miles sighed heavily again.

"I want to get down and kiss poor
Miles," whispered tender-hearted Pink Sunbonnet again.

Charley opened his astonished eyes. "I
never in all my life heard of a juror going
to kiss the prisoner. Don't think of it;"
and poor, patient little Pink composed herself again.

"Well, gentlemen of the jury," said Uncle Harry, "you must retire to consult upon
your verdict. It is a hard case. Try to do
right."

CHAPTER V.

THE jurors had a most stormy debate out in the back yard. Some of them declared that they never *would* say he was guilty, no matter what Jim Fuller, or even Uncle Harry himself, said; he had been such a kind, obliging boy. Each one had something pleasant to remember, and it seemed so mean to turn against him.

"But what else *can* we say?" said Charley Peterson, mournfully. "Miles acknowledges it himself, and Jim Fuller will always sneer, and say that our name 'Honorables' is a sham."

Finally, with heavy hearts, they came back all agreed, except the obstinate small juror, who declared she would never say anything against dear Miles.

" What is your verdict, gentlemen ? " said Paul.

" Guilty ! " said foreman Charley, trying to laugh, " but strongly recommended to mercy."

" Not guilty ! " interposed little Sunbonnet, bursting into tears.

" It's a lie in the second degree, any way," grumbled Dick ; " a sort of truth-slaughter ; not an out-and-out murder."

" It is just right," said Miles, with a brave effort at a smile. " What is the sentence ? "

Paul was anxiously communing with Uncle Harry.

" You must confess to Mr. Rinkel that you told him a falsehood," said Paul, presently, " and you can ask him to excuse you from telling how the fire happened, if you please, though we think it will be better if you persuade Jack to tell his story too."

5

"Yes, I'll tell him, if Uncle Harry says it's right," said poor Miles, eagerly. "It's hard to do it, but of course I ought to have *some* punishment. Oh, I'll be careful after this, boys! You'll see I'll never disgrace my badge again!" and he fastened the blue ribbon a little more securely.

"But there's something more," said Paul, turning away his head, and speaking very fast. "You are to be suspended from the club for a month!"

Miles started. This was a cruel blow, as his white lips plainly showed. Still he managed to smile again, and said, faintly, "It is all right."

"And the badge is to be taken off," said Paul, desperately, beckoning, with a red face, to some of the members.

No one stirred, and Miles himself unpinned it, with shaky fingers, and laid it on the table.

Then *such* an uproar! The Honorables

crowded around him with sympathy, hand-
shakings, and offers of friendship. Surely
never was prisoner, just sentenced, so honored before. Jim strode away angrily, to
ponder over the matter in bitterness of
heart. "Why was it that such good luck
always followed Miles, and turned even his
disgrace into a triumph?" Unhappy Jim!
was it *only* good luck?

But Miles was very far from being so ex-
ultant as Jim thought him. He escaped
from his friends as soon as possible, and
spent the afternoon closely locked in his
room, keenly realizing that his precious
badge was gone. At tea-time, when sister
Minnie knocked at the door, there was some
delay while he tucked away a suspiciously
damp handkerchief; and when she came in
with a tray of most wonderful dainties she
had been concocting all the afternoon, poor
Miles had not the heart to eat a morsel.

Perhaps some boys will think the punishment too hard; but could anything be too hard which taught Miles and those young Honorables the deceitful nature of a lie, and made them remember — wandering thoughtfully through the June day — how displeasing it was to Him who said that he who maketh or loveth a lie should in no wise enter into the holy city?

CHAPTER VI.

WEEK passed by. Mr. Rinkel had been told, and, as Charley Peterson said, had proved himself an "old trump." He forgave Miles, and forgave Jack, who came out like a man, and told his story, though weeping and trembling with penitence and fright.

"I guess you've been unhappy enough, boys," said old Rinkel, who'd been talking with Uncle Harry. "I'll let you off this time!"

But Miles had other trials still in store. Upon another of those loveliest June Saturdays, Georgie came pattering into Miles's room.

69

" Uncle Harry is going to give the club
a strawberry party this afternoon. An't you
glad, Miles? When are you going? and
when will I be old enough to be an Honorable? Say, Miles! Why don't you speak?"

Miles was thinking, " Why, I met Charley this morning, and he didn't say a word
about it. How strange! Oh! " — and his
head dropped into his hands, — " I know
now; I don't belong to the Honorables!"

"What's the matter, Miles?" persisted
Georgie.

" Go away, that's a good boy, Georgie!
I've got to take a great long walk this morning, — too long for *you*, Georgie," as the
boy began to plead. " Now, be good, and
I'll help you finish your wheelbarrow this
afternoon, and show you how to paint it."

" And not go to the party?" said Georgie,
with big eyes.

" No; my head aches," said Miles, which
was indeed the truth.

Rapidly through the streets went Miles, towards the open country. He wanted to cut across the fields, and take a long, long tramp by himself. He had a nervous fear that he should meet some of the boys, and they might look as if they pitied him. He couldn't bear that.

Well out in the suburbs, to his great annoyance he stumbled upon Jim Fuller, accompanied by his little satellite, Benny, both looking heated and tired.

" He who has a thousand friends has not a friend to spare,
But he who has *one* enemy shall meet him everywhere,"

said Miles, a little bitterly, and was sorry the minute after.

"I'm not a bit better pleased with the meeting than you are," retorted Jim, in his surliest mood.

"I beg your pardon, Jim," said Miles, frankly. "You'd forgive me if you knew how my head ached. But what's gone wrong with *you* this morning? Can I do anything to help you?"

"Well, now, that's quite brotherly," said Jim, with an unpleasant laugh; "but I don't know but it's natural enough, since we both belong to the *Dis*-honorables now."

Miles bit his lip. "I don't know that I'm very anxious to help you," said he, walking away coldly.

"I don't know that anybody asked you to, parson," said Jim, mimicking the tone, as he too went his way.

But Benny ran back in a minute.

"We've lost our cow, Miles," said he, hurriedly. "She got out some way in the night, and father is so angry with poor Jim; thinks he didn't put the bars up or something. You haven't seen her, have you, Miles?" said he, anxiously.

"No, indeed; and how tired you look, poor Benny!"

" We've been tramping since five o'clock,"
said Benny, beginning to cry.

" Here, Ben," cried Jim, with an angry
beckon, and frightened Ben ran after his
tyrant.

Miles went wearily on, thinking that the
June sunshine was sickly, and the birds
sang a great deal too loud,—made too much
of a fuss over their happiness. Poor sick-
hearted Miles!

On and on he walked, scarcely heeding
where he was going, with only a dull idea
in his head that he was getting very tired,
when he was suddenly brought to his sen-
ses by a long " Moo-oo!" To be sure,
there, at the edge of the wood, composedly
whisking her tail, stood Mr. Fuller's cow,
two or three miles from home.

" What shall I do now?" thought Miles,
putting his hand to his perplexed, aching
head. " If I go and tell Jim, perhaps
before he gets here she will stray off some-

where else. Besides, Jim was very tired,
and that poor Benny,— he'd make him
come too. I must try to drive her back
myself."

It would be too long a story to tell how
painfully Miles labored with the stubborn
old cow; how sometimes she wouldn't go
at all, and then again would suddenly start
full trot down some little by-path, the June
sun all the time mounting higher and higher, and shining with a blinding glare on
the dusty road.

"One would almost think it was Jim
himself," said poor Miles in despair. "It
seems just like a nightmare; I shall never
get home!"

And indeed it would have been some-
what doubtful — with his head aching as
if it would split — if it had not occurred to
him to go through Mr. Brown's farm, and
cut off half the distance at least.

It was very hard to keep mischievous old

Susan just in the narrow track through the nicely planted fields; but everything must have an end, and at last the feat was accomplished, and Miles thankfully found himself almost home.

As he turned the last corner into the long village street, he was startled by a rough exclamation, and there again was Jim, coming rapidly towards him, with poor draggled Benny limping in the rear.

" Indeed! " cried Jim, his face in a blaze. " So I'm indebted to you for this morning's tramp! *You* let her out; I was almost sure of it from the first, just for revenge, eh? Oh, what a deceitful — "

" Hush, Jim," said Miles, wiping his forehead with a trembling hand; " you don't know what you are saying. I've driven old Susan all the way from Pine Hollow, just to save you the trouble, and this is the way you thank me."

" I don't believe a word of it ! " cried

Jim, ashamed to be convinced. " You drove
her home because you thought you'd get
into trouble if you kept her any longer."

" Oh, Jimmy, don't talk so to poor good
Miles ! " cried little Benny.

" Are *you* going over too, Ben ? " said
unhappy Jim, bursting into passionate grief;
and leaving Benny to make his peace as
best he could, Miles went staggering home.

In at the garden gate he stumbled, almost
blind. " I never can get up stairs," he
thought, and tottering a few steps further,
he threw himself down under a great elm
tree by the garden fence.

Now the little breezes whispered together,
" Let us fan his hot head ; " the mother
birds overhead scolded the baby robins lest
they should twitter too loud, and the flowers
elbowed each other, and said, " Let him lay
his head on my breast."

So poor Miles, utterly exhausted, fell into
a sweet sleep, — dreamed that he was an

Honorable again; dreamed that his twenty shillings bought a perfect library of histories and travels,—and finally came slowly back to consciousness, greatly comforted and refreshed.

"A quarter of the time is passed, any way," said Miles hopefully, remembering his dream. "In three weeks I shall be a member again."

But what were those angry voices just outside the fence? Miles rose on his elbow to listen.

"It *was* you; don't try to cheat me!" said farmer Brown, angrily. "My Sam saw you. He thought it was bold in you, any way, to go through our field, but he thought of course you weren't such a heathen as to leave the bars down. There were pigs and cows,—I couldn't count the cattle trampling down my young corn, ruining my crops; you shall pay for it, you scamp!"

"I — I didn't do it," stammered a voice that seemed very familiar.

Could it be Jim Fuller's? Miles sprang to his feet, put his eye to a knot-hole, and sure enough, there was farmer Brown with his hand wound in Jim's collar, while wretched little Benny, in an agony of grief, clung to his coat behind.

"Come along!" cried Mr. Brown, as Jim hung back, clutching at every rail of the fence. "You shall go before a lawyer, and if you've got a cent of pocket-money you shall pay it for damages. I've scolded you youngsters enough; it's time you had a lesson you'll remember!"

Miles had a dozen thoughts in as many seconds. Could it have been I who left the bars down? I'm always so careful; and yet my head ached so — I can not be sure. If it was, though, I needn't speak. Let that sulky, ungenerous Jim suffer a little; he didn't spare me any. Nobody is asking *me* anything about it. I needn't send either a lie or a truth to the door. Didn't they say it was better to keep silent sometimes, and quite right too?"

"Ah, yes, Miles!" said his better angel. "It is right not to tell evil of another unnecessarily; but how is it when through your not speaking another is to suffer unjustly? What is your silence then?"

"A cowardly lie!" said Miles, putting his foot on the fence; but he drew back.

"I've had enough disgrace," said he, bitterly. "If I should be taken before a real lawyer now, what will the whole town think of me? I shall never get over it."

"Don't take poor Jim's money," sobbed Benny. "He's worked so hard to earn it for the 'Fourth.' He's only got two dollars—"

"Hush, you ninny!" cried Jim; "you don't know that I've got a cent."

"Two dollars, eh?" said Farmer Brown. "Well, that's better than nothing."

A wail arose from Benny. "Then we won't have any cannon, Jim!"

Just then a boy dropped down at Mr. Brown's feet as if he came out of the clouds, saying,—

"It was *I* did it.   Let him go."

"You!" said farmer Brown, looking into the honest blue eyes. "Did you drive a black and white cow through—"

"Yes, yes!" cried Miles hastily, "I did. I don't know how I happened to leave the bars down. I'm sorry, and here's all my money," said he with a little gulp, emptying his pockets, and counting out by ten cents and five cents the "History" and "Travels" into Mr. Brown's horny hand. "There," said he, with a heavy sigh, "it's all I have. Please don't take me to the lawyer."

"Well," said Mr. Brown, carefully counting it, "twenty shillings, eh? Perhaps that

will cover damages. You seem an honest
boy, and I'll let you go this time. I would
not take it," continued he, turning the
money a little uneasily from one hand to
another, "but you see I've let off a good
many with only a scolding, and it's no good.
I must try something else, my young gentlemen, if I mean to have any crops this
year;" and farmer Brown went his way.

Jim came up to Miles, who was leaning,
very pale, against the fence.

"I suppose," said he, "according to all
the old Sunday-school books, I ought to get
down and lick the dust off your shoes, and
say that I'm the meanest boy in creation,
and you're a saint, and ask very humbly if
you'd condescend to shake hands with me,
and teach me how to be good as you are?
But I can't do it," said Jim, fiercely. "It's
just as much as I can do to stand all this.
I suppose it's kind, but I'd rather you'd
have knocked me over twenty times. I can't

6

thank you ; but I'll say this, I won't meddle
with you again, if you tell a hundred lies.
Come, Benny !" and unhappy Jim went on
his way. Let us hope that he came to a
better mind.

Miles was still leaning disconsolately
against the fence, when he suddenly felt
something thrust into his listless fingers.
If he had turned quicker he might have
caught Benny's meager little hand. As it
was, the boy was a dozen paces off in a
twinkling. "I wish I had more, Miles,"
he sobbed, "but I haven't;" and Benny
was gone, while Miles was much distressed
to find two little crumpled postage stamps
left in his hand.

Afternoon came, and Miles faithfully per-
formed his promise to Georgie. The wheelbarrow was fast approaching completion,
and they were just discussing the best color
to paint it, when Georgie started to his feet.
"What's that noise, Miles ?" and away he

clattered to the gate, to be back in a minute.
—"Oh, Miles, it's the Honorables on their
way to Uncle Harry's!"

Miles shrunk back, for there was a clatter
of many feet, and a perfect hubbub of happy
voices.

"It's cruel in them to all march past
here," thought the poor boy. "They often
go the other way."

"Miles, I believe they're coming here,"
cried Georgie, excitedly.

Miles went farther back in the shrubbery.

"Oh, if they want that flag sister Minnie
was going to make, tell them it isn't quite
done. Hurry, Georgie!" For the Honorables had halted in front of the house, and
now there were loud cries of "Miles!"
"Miles!"

Miles wouldn't stir.

"Here he is!" cried Georgie, flinging
wide the gate, and the happy group poured
quickly in.

At the head walked, or danced, little Mabel Thornton, bearing a basket of flowers, in the center of which lay a new blue badge, with the letters " H. C." glittering in unusual magnificence.

Miles, trying to escape, was surrounded by the whole tumultuous party. There were hand-shakings and hurrahs that brought Minnie and Jenny Seabright out on the piazza.

" You didn't jump the wrong way this time, did you, old fellow ? " cried Paul.

" Don't look so innocent and bewildered," laughed Charley. " We know all about it. Didn't Ben tell little Phil, and Phil tell me, and we all tell Uncle Harry ? "

" And you're pardoned out," cried Dick, turning a most undignified somersault. "Dear old fellow, you are an Honorable again ! "

" Be careful with that big mouth of yours

when you smile, Dick," cried Charley. "I declare it most met behind just now!"

The happy Honorables burst into light-hearted laughter, while Pink Sunbonnet gave Charley a timid pull. "To be sure," said Charley, lifting her in his arms, "and here's Miss Pink, whose sister has made you a brand new badge, because the old one looked as if you'd been caught in the *rain* some time. Allow us—" and Pink's little fingers carefully fastened it in its place.

Miles's blue eyes were all in a mist. He opened his mouth, but couldn't speak.

"Hurrah!" cried little Georgie.

"Hurrah!" cried sister Minnie and Jenny from the piazza.

"Hurrah!" cried the young Honorables in deafening chorus.

The small juror conferred anxiously with Charley.

"Not the least objection now in the world," said Charley, lifting her again.

"Dear Miles," said she, softly patting his cheek, "I've saved all my strawberries for *you;*". and little Pink Sunbonnet *kissed* him!

MISS PEACOCK'S DIARY.

DEDICATED TO *SOME* YOUNG PERSONS WHO MAY
LIKE TO SEE HOW THEIR PRIVATE
THOUGHTS WOULD APPEAR
IN PRINT.

87

MISS PEACOCK'S DIARY.

CHAPTER I.

A STEP HIGHER.

RIVERSIDE, June 7. I have found out lately that a great many very distinguished people have kept diaries, and it has occurred to me that it is a duty I owe myself, and perhaps the world, to keep a record of *my* daily life. Aunt Jane always told me she knew I was born to be famous,—such beauty and talents could never be hid under a bushel. She was sure I would make the whole family celebrated. Poor, awkward old soul! she never made any figure in the world herself,

but she had very good sense, and great pen-
etration, as one may see from her estimate
of *me*.

It is a great comfort to me to think I was
always so kind and considerate to Aunt
Jane, now that she is gone, poor creature!
To be sure, that very impertinent Fanny
Blythe said to me one day,—

"Lotty" (she always calls me "Lotty,"
although she knows I prefer to be called by
my whole name, "Charlotte Adelaide"),—
"Lotty, I shouldn't think you would ask
for another new dress while your aunt's
best bombazine looks so rusty and thin.
Why don't you insist on her buying something once in a while for herself?"

I was very angry with Fanny, but I am
never unlady-like, and did not forget myself then. I had been reading in a lovely
volume of poems that very morning this
line,—"The lady rose and *stabbed* him with
her angry eyes." So I rose, and tried the

same thing upon Fanny. (I have splendid eyes!) I must confess, however, that Fanny didn't seem to feel it. She only laughed, and asked me if I " had a stitch in my side."

It is very disagreeable to associate with low-bred, unsympathetic people. Now she could never understand, though I told her a thousand times, that Aunt Jane's highest gratification seemed to be in seeing me dressed like a lady. Often on a Sunday morning when I put on my green silk, and my lace bonnet with drooping white lilies, she looked as if she could hardly contain herself with pride and delight. How glad I am I was always kind to her. I always used to let her dress me on Sundays, or any great occasion, it gratified her so; and then when we walked to church,—for I never was too proud to walk with her even in her old bombazine,— how pleased she was with the notice we attracted. I remember learning at school the moon had no brilliancy of her own, but shone with a reflected light from the sun. In the same way, I think I may describe Aunt Jane as a kind of moon, all her importance being reflected from *me*.

As I said before, I am very glad I was so kind to her. I remember I always told her that her name should go down to posterity with mine; when I wrote a history of my life, I would certainly put her in: and if that wasn't noble and generous in me, when you remember how awkward and plain and commonplace Aunt Jane was, then I should like to know what generosity is!

But I have talked enough about my past life. I have spoken of Aunt Jane as I promised, and I will say still further that she was obliging and good-natured, and I suppose I might say generous, for she never denied me anything if she had a cent. But why she didn't lay by a sum for me every year, when she knew I was a penniless orphan, and her annuity expired at her

death, I can not see. She certainly did
not do me justice there, but I have tried to
forgive her. I forgive Fanny too, who
says,—

"I don't see that you have any one to
blame but yourself. It took all your aunt
could rake and scrape to buy your green
silks, and blue silks, and ribbons, and folde-
rols."

How blunt she is! One would have certainly thought she would have had a little
tenderness and sympathy when I had just
met with such a loss.

I was quite heart-broken the day Aunt
Jane died, but I now see it was all for the
best, and ordered for my highest good. My
Uncle Willoughby, to whom Aunt Jane
wrote the week before she died, came for
me yesterday, and brought me to his own
home at Riverside.

It is just the loveliest place! a beautiful
old-fashioned house, but with every modern

comfort: broad piazzas on two sides, and beautiful grounds, with flowers and green lawns, vases and statues. I feel as if I were a princess just come home to my true inheritance. It almost seems as if I should have been here years ago, and Aunt Jane had been a little unfair in living so long. However, I will not say anything evil of the dead, no matter what reason I have. When I think of what might be called her selfishness in keeping me with her in that humble life, I must also remember her temptations; how she idolized me, and how I was, in short, her sun.

Now, I feel that my true life is beginning at last. As soon as I get a little more settled in my pretty room, I shall begin to think how I shall best work out my destiny, and make myself famous.

There is only one thing disagreeable at Uncle Willoughby's, and that is the number of children. I never could bear children, and I do not intend to be troubled with these. I shall not take the slightest notice of the four or five younger ones, for with the least encouragement they are sure to be always teasing and hanging around.

There is Fred, just about my own age. I think I had better make friends with him, for there is a look about his eyes that reminds me of Fanny Blythe, as if he might be saucy, and a dangerous enemy. Yes, I certainly shall be very polite to *him*.

Then Ida is a little younger, but seems amiable, and I think could be easily led. She can probably be made very useful helping me dress, and sewing on some of my buttons and tapes.

Louis is the next, — a little deformed boy, to whom I shall give candy once in a while, but shall not encourage him so that he will ever expect me to read to him or tell him stories as the rest of the family do. I wonder if they don't know they are spoiling him and making him very selfish.

As for the rest of the children, they are not worth describing. Oh, I forgot Seymour, but then he isn't here. He is at college, and some day will be a minister. How stupid! That one thing has set me against him. If he were going to be a merchant, or lawyer, or member of Congress, and live in a grand house, and be somebody! and yet Ida seems to think him a wonder, and I never tell her any stories about my heroes who have done anything very brave or noble, but she will exclaim, — " That's just like Seymour!"

I don't believe he is anything but a great awkward booby, with tolerably good intentions. I wonder if he will not be surprised when he sees me with what Fanny will call my " company manners; " I am very graceful, and have a great deal of style. Perhaps I shall be able to do him a great deal of good when he comes home in vacation. I think it will be a great advantage to *all*

the children to have any one so graceful
and lady-like in the house; and how pleasant it will be, by and by, when Uncle
comes to thank me for the happy influence
I have had in his family!

That disagreeable Fanny Blythe tried to
make me think the obligation was all on
my side, and that uncle was wonderfully
kind to adopt me, and promise me the
same allowance he gave Ida. But I think
in a year's time he will feel himself more
than paid, and will know that he has taken
a treasure into the house. Besides, when
I become famous, only think what honor I
shall confer upon the whole family! The
debt will be on the other side then, beyond
question. People will come from all around
to see the place where I live, just as they
now visit the home of Charlotte Bronte,
and all uncle's family will bless the day
when I came to Riverside.

7

CHAPTER II.

JUNE 24. I am very unhappy indeed, and my only consolation is in knowing that all gifted persons have been subject to fits of depression, and have always been a mark for the envy and ill-treatment of the world.

I just begin to realize what I lost in Aunt Jane. No one here seems to think I am anything remarkable, while *she* never had a doubt that I could do whatever I had a mind to. The only obstacle to my becoming very famous, we both thought, was because I had so many gifts it was hard to tell which to cultivate first. Sometimes I've quite decided to be a great musician, and play so splendidly that everybody would be enchanted and melted to tears, and I haven't given that up yet, although Fanny Blythe has tried in every way to discourage me.

Now Fanny plays on the church organ, in that little one-street village where Aunt Jane lived, and though it is only a big music-box with a make-believe swell, she is just as conceited about it as if it had four banks of keys and no end of pedals. I won't say but what Fanny plays very well for a girl of her age, but *I* have exquisite musical taste, and she never satisfies me.

One Sunday I thought I would show her what good playing really was. I had been reading an account of a great organist over in Germany, who could tell a story in music. First he imitated a storm, the wind coming up, the pattering of the rain, the thunder, and then made his audience understand, just by music, that a little child was lost in the woods and was crying. It was so natural that they all were in tears before they knew it.

I hadn't the least doubt but I could produce the same effect upon our organ. I practiced a little upon the piano, and got the wind and thunder very well, and thought I would leave the rest to the inspiration of the moment, as most geniuses do. So I proposed it to Fanny, thinking she would be greatly pleased.

" You will see the congregation in tears," said I, " before I am half through."

" I shall see them run out of the house before you're a quarter through," said she, in her blunt way.

" You are envious, Fanny," said I quietly, " but that is what we must always expect."

" Who are ' we,' pray ? ' said Fanny.

" The geniuses, the eagles who soar out of sight of the common barn-yard fowls."

Fanny laughed till she was like a lobster.

I stood quiet and lady-like till she was quite through.

"Maybe you know nothing about the natural history of eagles."

"I've heard of them," gasped Fanny, "but how about the *peacocks?*"

Then it was my turn to get red. I burst into tears, the joke was so exceedingly coarse and heartless. Could I help my unfortunate name?

"Forgive me, Lotty," cried Fanny, sober in a minute, when she saw what she had done.

If she had had any tact at all, she would, at such a moment, have called me "Charlotte Adelaide" (my first name is certainly very aristocratic and pleasing), and I told her so.

"Forgive me, Charlotte Adelaide, then," said she, but her eyes twinkled, and I would not be consoled till she had promised to let me play.

Sunday morning I was there bright and early.

" Won't you practice a little first ? " asked Fanny, anxiously. She always has to practice, poor soul ! but I felt confidence in myself, and declined.

The people assembled, the minister was in his place ; there wasn't a sound beyond a June bug bumping his head against the wall, and I began.

The organ didn't sound quite as well as I expected. I suppose I shouldn't have thought of producing such grand effects upon such a miserable instrument, but I did my best. The wind had risen, and I had thundered once, when Fanny gave my sleeve a pull.

" You are making dreadful discord," she said.

I had expected she would be jealous of my success, and so took no notice of the interruption.

"Everybody is looking around," said Fanny again.

"Nothing more than I expected," said I.

"*Do* stop! they'll think it is I."

"So much the better for you," said I, going on with the crying of the child, which I would have finished to my entire satisfaction if that stupid organ-boy hadn't stopped blowing the bellows.

I was a little disappointed in the effect, for no one was in tears, but I had evidently made a sensation, for people were exchanging looks, and there were one or two whispers.

I said no one was crying, but I ought to have excepted Fanny Blythe, who was behind the organ, breaking her heart. I was quite disgusted with her want of generosity, and said to her,—

"Fanny, do you know what is the matter with you?"

"Yes, Charlotte Adelaide," said she, disagreeably; "I shall be very much blamed for letting you play on the organ, when you didn't know anything about it. Why, if our cat had walked over the keys she would have played a better voluntary than you did."

I didn't get angry with her, but only said quietly,—"Hadn't you better tell the truth, my dear? You are envious, that is all, and I will tell you a good definition of envy I have lately read: 'Envy is that feeling by which we punish ourselves for being inferior to others.' Doesn't that exactly suit your case?"

She wouldn't answer, she was so sulky.

"Well," said I, thinking perhaps I had better say something to comfort her, "I'll promise you this, if the committee come this week to ask me to take your place at the organ, I promise you I'll decline their proposal."

Instead of being touched by this generos-

ity, she only gave a little giggle, and said,—
"What an absurd girl you are!"

I remember the sermon that morning was something about not thinking more highly of ourselves than we ought to think, and it did seem so appropriate for Fanny, though I'm not at all sure she took it to heart.

I don't know why I keep going back to that humble life, but that Fanny Blythe just seems to haunt me. I'm so glad she wasn't here yesterday, for I know she would have enjoyed a little mortification I had.

I had been telling uncle about my very fine voice; I could sing on the high notes like a bird, and if I had a few lessons I was sure I should be a second Jenny Lind or Patti. I should soon earn a thousand dollars a night, and not only take care of myself, but make the whole family wealthy. Uncle laughed, and said I should take lessons immediately of Ida's teacher, Mr. Mo-

rensi, who would come that very day,—
that was yesterday.

He didn't come till afternoon, and by
that time I had quite made up my mind to
become famous as a singer. I should have
bouquets thrown at my feet with diamonds
for dew-drops, I should dress like a queen,
I should give away great sums in charity,
and be universally beloved.

Imagine my disappointment, then, when
Mr. Morensi tried my voice, and said I could
never be more than an ordinary singer. My
voice was thin and of small compass, nothing to be compared to Ida's; still he thought
he could improve it very much.

I thanked him, and said if I couldn't be
a great singer I wouldn't be any at all, and
then ran away to my room, and cried all
the afternoon. It is so vexatious, too, that I
told Fred anything about my brilliant plans.
He has called me nothing but "Patti"
ever since, and it is so disagreeable, now

that I have given it all up. Yes, I have
determined to think no more about it. That
little quarter of a talent shall be wrapped
up in its napkin again, out of sight. Thank
fortune, though, I have more gifts than one.

CHAPTER III.

JUNE 27. I have had another great grief. I have often heard that every rose must have its thorn. I wish it were just as true that every thorn must have its rose. Now I only have one big thorn of a mortification after another, and nothing pleasant with it. Ever since giving up being a great singer I've been thinking,—"Why not be a sculptor like Harriet Hosmer, or a painter like Rosa Bonheur?" Seeing one of Fred's drawings lately, reminded me that Aunt Jane always thought I had wonderful talent in that direction. I took several sketches of our neighborhood, which, when I told her what they were, she

108

recognized in a minute, with tears of pride
and delight; besides, many and many a doll
I have made out of putty and dried in the
sun, showing that I could easily learn to
make models out of clay. However, after a
great deal of thought, I made my final de-
cision, this morning, to be a painter.

I didn't begin the day very pleasantly,
for when I came down stairs, full of my new
plans, aunt wanted me to dust the parlors,
because Ann was sick, and then she said I
must do a little sewing, and not spend all
my days so idly.

It never seems to occur to aunt that I am
not an ordinary girl, and should not be
kept hemming handkerchiefs when I could
be doing something of so much more importance. So I just let the parlors go, and
carried the sewing up to Ida.

" Why, mamma has given me some of
my own to do," said she.

" Well, you'll have time for it all, I

guess," said I, very pleasantly, for I am always good-natured.

"It makes my shoulder ache to sew so much," said the disobliging child.

"Don't fret now, my dear," said I, "that's such a bad habit. Just keep right on sewing, and the first thing you know it will be done. You must cultivate a habit of looking on the bright side; it will be worth everything to you." But seeing she still hesitated, I concluded to flatter her by taking her into my confidence. "You must know," said I, "that I am going to be a great artist, and now, while you are just pulling your needle in and out through this easy work, I shall be down on the back piazza, working very hard at my drawing. I shall be very famous one of these days, and with the first money I earn I'll buy you a gold watch!"

I am generous to a fault, and one would suppose she might have appreciated this

SKETCHING

utter forgetfulness of self, but she is a dull
child, fond of present ease, and never sees
an inch beyond her nose. So she only
looked as if she were going to cry, — so tiresome! and I ran off and left her. Discontented people are so disagreeable! I am almost always cheerful.

But now about my drawing. I went to
Fred's room, took some of his pencils and
paper, and then settled myself on the piazza. As Rosa Bonheur is so celebrated for
her animal paintings, I thought I would
follow her example, and make my first attempt on the cat. I made Loucy come out
and hold her, for she wouldn't keep still a
minute.

I may as well say here that Loucy is
perfectly fascinated with me, thinks I know
everything, and am the most beautiful person in the world. I *am* a great contrast to
him, poor little Humpy! He is generally
only too happy to do anything for me, but

this morning he must needs be unreasonable too, and try me almost beyond endurance.

We had just got nicely settled, with the cat in the very best position, when he must want to move,—said the "sun was creeping around."

Now Ida, who always spoils him, would have jumped right up and moved him. But *I* thought it was a good time to teach him self-control. So I moved his crutches out of his reach, and forbade him to stir a finger till I had sketched the entire cat.

He was very still about five minutes, not a second more, and then he interrupted me again.

"Cousin Charlotte Adelaide" (I have taught him to be very particular with my name, and he doesn't dare disobey me), "it makes my head ache dreadfully to sit in the sun."

I didn't take any notice at first, but after a while I began to tell him a story of a

Spartan boy who had been taught to despise suffering. He had stolen a fox, and when he was in danger of being discovered he hid it inside his vest. There it gnawed his breast, and almost tore out his heart, but the brave boy didn't cry out, nor move a muscle of his face. "That was splendid," said I, "but it is very babyish and unmanly to make such a fuss over a little pain."

Louey colored very much, and then I forgot all about him till I had the cat almost done. Then I heard a step coming, and thinking it might be aunt, and knowing she doesn't always think as I do about governing the children, I jumped up and moved Louey. It turned out to be only Fred.

"What are you about now, Miss Charlotte Adelaide Patti?" said he.

I didn't take any notice of his impudence, but held up my cat a little triumphantly, perhaps, for I had every reason to be proud of it.

8

"What in the world is it?" said Fred, turning it every way, upside down, sideways, till I was quite out of patience.

"Don't be so disagreeable, Fred; you know well enough what it is."

"Oh, yes," drawled he at last, "I see now. It's a study of vegetables,—a crookneck squash set up on four radishes,—and very good too, now I see it."

Loucy gave a half laugh, ending in a little sob, while *I* burst into tears.

Of course Fred didn't pay the least attention to me if he thought anything ailed Loucy. They make such a baby of the child!

"Why, what's the matter, small boy?" said he, so tenderly. "How white you are! What have you been about?"

Loucy gave a little look at me, and I just said, as if to myself,—"let the fox tear his heart out, and never complained."

"What?" said Fred, turning very quickly;

but I pretended to be looking for something, and Louey shut his little mouth very firmly and wouldn't say a word.

" Seems to me you're both very stupid," said Fred, who hasn't much patience, " but it's plain enough Louey is sick, and I shall carry him into the house."

As they passed me, Louey whispered, " I didn't complain, did I, cousin Charlotte Adelaide ? "

I shook my head.

" Am I like the Spartan boy now ? " he cried, just as they were going into the door ; but I was busy with my drawing again, and didn't take the trouble to answer him. What plagues children are ! I suppose he will bother me about that for weeks.

But I'm not half through with my troubles. Just after they had left me in peace, out came aunt, looking greatly displeased. Some company had been in, and there had been two grains of dust on the center-table, and a chair out of place I suppose. Such a trifling thing for aunt to be angry about; but she knew I hadn't minded her, and so she read me a long lecture on selfishness and disobedience, and I, not wishing to lose my temper, just thought about something else till she got through.

They say that getting in a passion injures the complexion, and I am very careful about it on that account, for I have the fairest skin in the world, with a little pink color in my cheeks like a sea-shell.

Well, in the end Aunt Willoughby sent me up to my room to stay till dinner-time. Not so much of a punishment as she supposes. I spent at least an hour very pleasantly looking at myself in the glass, and trying on all my pretty ribbons. Colors are very becoming to me, and it's very provoking to have to wear black for Aunt Jane. But, thanks to my good disposition, I don't fret about it, as some would, especially as,

at times, when I put on my pensive expression, I think it makes me more interesting.

After I had looked at my pretty eyes and
hair and cheeks as long as I wished, I
stole across to Ida's room, and found she
hadn't much more than half my work done.
I just made some little remark about her
laziness, and she was all ready to cry again.
How hard it is to live with people so easily
upset.

As I was leaving her I chanced to see
the corner of a book peeping out under a
handkerchief, and guessed how the time
had gone.

I slipped it into my pocket. " I shall take
this away, Ida," I said, " till your work is
done."

When I was back in my room I settled
myself in the big chair, and thought I
would read a while. I certainly needed
rest after my morning's walk. I thought,
of course, it was some good novel Ida was

hiding so carefully, but there, when I drew it out it was only the Bible! so I threw it down, and have been writing in my journal ever since.

How poky it makes girls to be always reading the Bible and trying to be good! Now Ida is no companion at all for *me*, and I have disliked Fanny Blythe a hundred times more than ever since she joined the church.

But I won't think any more about these disagreeable things. To-morrow we expect visitors, and a very fine artist will be among them. I intend to leave some of my sketches around carelessly, and see how he is affected when they first catch his eyes. I must dress myself carefully in case he insists upon seeing the person who has shown so much talent.

June 28. I am not half so happy here as I was at Aunt Jane's. There is so much envy and ill-feeling in the family, such con-

stant determination to mortify and break
my spirit.

For instance, this morning I had just ar-
ranged my drawings on the center-table,
when in came aunt to see that everything
was in order. Now I don't like to call
aunt ill-natured, but how else can I describe
her when she said, —

" Why, Ann, how came you to leave this
rubbish here ? Take it away to the nursery.
Oh, are they yours, Charlotte ? " she said,
as I sprang forward. " Carry them up to
your own room."

But I didn't; I put them in a portfolio
of choice engravings, which I knew would
be turned over in the course of the day.
How differently she would have acted if
they had been Fred's ; she only wants her
own children to be noticed.

The company came, and I had one moment of triumph when the painter first
caught sight of me. I was dressed all in

white, except a black sash, and a ribbon at
my throat, and my soft light hair was curled
in beautiful ringlets. It had taken me
ever since breakfast to arrange it. I stood
on the piazza, leaning gracefully against
the railing, with one hand on Ida's shoulder. I kept Ida by me because she is sal-
low and round-shouldered, and I knew I
should look so much prettier by contrast.

Pretty soon there were steps on the piazza,
but I didn't look up, even when some one
exclaimed (it was Mr. Barnard, the artist), —

" What a lovely girl, and what rare hair!
it is like the halo in some of the old pictures of the saints! "

" Hush! " said my disagreeable aunt;
" she knows it too well already."

She didn't suppose I heard that, but I
did, and I heard Mr. Barnard say, in a lower
tone, —

" Is it possible ? and she looks so unconscious. I should like to paint her some day, though; she is almost perfect."

I still pretended not to hear, but soon stole away up stairs to look at myself. He certainly was right about it; I was very lovely. But this shows how envious every one else is in the house. No one but that little goose Louey has told me I was even pretty, since I came.

But now comes my mortification. When I came down again, they were just turning over the engravings, and I hid behind the curtains of the nearest window.

" What's this ? " said Mr. Barnard, holding up my Roman warrior done in crayons

" That," said that disgusting Fred, who hasn't forgiven me for taking his drawing-paper without leave, — " that seems to be a likeness of our charcoal peddler, when he hadn't washed for a week; and this," said he, taking up my " sleeping infant," " is a faithful copy of Mrs. Green's youngest, who has the rickets,—all head, you see; and here, I declare, is the squash and radishes too! Oh, cousin Charlotte Adelaide!" and he burst into one of his horse laughs.

Mr. Barnard laughed too, and aunt said,—

" Why, I told her to put away that rubbish, but the poor child seems to have an idea she's a genius, and that these scrawls have wonderful merit."

I was just burning up with shame, but I didn't dare to come out.

" How old is she?" asked Mr. Barnard.

" Almost fifteen," said Fred.

" The case isn't very encouraging then," said Mr. Barnard, laughing again. " These might have been done by a child half that age."

The worst of it is, he went on flattering Fred greatly about some of *his* sketches, and the boy, who was conceited enough before, will be just intolerable now. He is going to take lessons of Mr. Barnard, and I suppose the house will be filled with his daubs and scrawls.

I am not at all convinced but what I could be a fine artist yet, but I shall meet with such ridicule if I go on now, that I am determined to give it up for the present. Perhaps, after all, my true career is to be that of an author. I have always written with the greatest ease and fluency. I wonder I haven't thought of it before. I shall write a book immediately: I would begin to-day, but I am a little low-spirited.

Aunt has been very much troubled about Louey, who has been feverish and restless all day, and does not seem at all well. I went in to see him a little while ago, to tell him how much more I should respect him, how much more *manly* it would be, if he didn't tell about sitting in the sun, and fret and make a great fuss about a little headache.

"I haven't complained at all, cousin Charlotte Adelaide," said he. "Will you think I'm anything like that brave Spartan boy?" How bright and eager his eyes looked.

"Yes, a little, but remember, if you tell about the sun, that will be downright baby-ish."

"I never will," said Loucy; "but don't go away to the company yet. Let me put my hand just once on one of your pretty curls."

But I thought he might rumple it, and said, —

"No, I must go now. Don't you know I've been very kind to come in and see you at all?"

"Yes, I know it," said he, lying back, with a long sigh.

I wish he hadn't looked quite so dismal as I went away. Aunt's children, all but Fred, are so low-spirited, and I'm so kind-hearted it makes me uneasy. My example of constant cheerfulness ought to begin to have some effect, I think.

I wonder what sort of a body Seymour will be? He will soon be home now.

CHAPTER IV.

THE THIRD TALENT.

JULY 7. We have had a very dull, tiresome week, on account of Loucy's illness. One night they even thought he would die, and nobody but I and the younger children went to bed in the house. I am of a very delicate nervous temperament, and knew I must take good care of myself or I should be sick too. Besides, loss of sleep is so bad for the eyes, and just ruins the complexion.

Nevertheless, I was not permitted to rest in peace. Aunt called me up at one o'clock at night, and told me to come into Loucy's room.

He was talking in a very wild way about

the sun burning him, and a fox eating his head; then he'd call my name, and beg me to take it away, for he couldn't bear it any longer.

"What does he mean? What have you been putting in his head?" said my aunt, very sternly.

But I was very innocent, and told her I "had never heard of such a thing as a fox eating any one's head," which was very true.

Aunt wasn't at all satisfied with what I said, and looked at me so suspiciously that I felt very uncomfortable indeed.

"You could tell if you wished to," said she, in her coldest tones. "You may go back to your room."

So I went, and only the thought of spoiling my eyes kept me from a hearty fit of crying.

How I do miss Aunt Jane! she was the only one who fully appreciated me. How

I do wish she were here just one hour, if it were only long enough to mend my stockings!

Aunt Willoughby has made such an absurd rule, that we must learn to do our own mending. Ida used to do the most of it for me, but this last week she has spent in the nursery, helping keep the children still, for the least noise distressed Loucy.

No one knows how lonely I've been, for even Fred has been busy, and pays me no more attention than if I were a fly buzzing on the window-pane. He carries King Loucy hours· every day, and then is too tired to walk with me or listen to a word I say.

It certainly is a very sad world, and I have thought a great deal lately that I shan't know much more happiness till I get to heaven.

July 7. P. M. Ida has just come in, and says there is a decidedly favorable change

in Loucy, and on the whole I'm glad. If
he had died I should always have felt a little uneasy about that morning.

July 24. Everything looks brighter this
beautiful summer morning. Loucy is almost as well as ever, and Seymour is home
at last. I have been very agreeably disappointed in Seymour, who, instead of being
an awkward booby, is perfectly self-pos-
sessed, with the most pleasing manners in
the world ; so different from Fred, and yet
I believe I am more afraid of him. He has
such a strange look sometimes, which I
have studied over a great deal, and can not
in the least understand. I noticed it last
evening as Ida and I were walking through
the shrubbery towards the house, and he sat
on the piazza, looking miles away into the
red sunset, with that peaceful far-away
look.

"What are you looking at?" said I, almost impatiently.

"Hush!" said Ida, drawing me away
again, and speaking very low. "I know
what you mean, but we never trouble him
when he looks so. The first time we ever
noticed it was a year ago, when he was so
sick. He had been studying too hard, and
came home with brain fever. After he had
just lived through that, he had the most
terrible pains in his head and eyes; neural-
gia, I believe they called it; and Dr. Brown
told him it was very doubtful whether he
could ever study again, or be a minister, as
he hoped. This was a thousand times
worse than the pain. Seymour had talked
about being a minister ever since he was a
little boy, and we thought this would just
break his heart. But he only asked to be
all alone a little while, and then he was just
as cheerful and pleasant as ever. But from
that time I began to notice that look. Sometimes he wouldn't hear when I first spoke
to him."

"But what is it?" said I again; "what is he thinking about?"

"I will tell you what papa wrote to May Hampton, who, you know, is Seymour's most intimate friend. May wrote first to papa, asking all about Seymour, and 'how he bore such a cruel disappointment?' and papa wrote back just these words: 'He endures as seeing Him who is invisible.'"

"You mean, then, that when he has that look he is thinking so earnestly of God, and what will please him, that he almost believes he sees him?"

"Yes," said Ida, with a ridiculously reverent air.

"Oh, pshaw!" said I; "don't be so solemn. I don't believe a word of it. He is day-dreaming, building air-castles; I do it myself, often."

The absurd child colored violently, and drew herself up, as if I had hurt her feelings. I haven't any patience with such over-sensitiveness, and I told her so: but she wouldn't talk any more; she had drawn herself in, like a turtle into its shell.

But somehow what she said—though I don't believe a word of it—makes me uneasy. I know I have a great many excellent qualities, and I had been thinking how pleasant it would be to have Seymour at home; some one who could understand me, and sympathize with me fully; but our goodness seems very different. I know he has shown courage and endurance, but there's something I don't understand about it. I like the Spartan boy better.

Nevertheless, I have been quite anxious that he should have a good opinion of me, and I surprised Loucy by reading to him an hour this morning, and even letting him lay his foolish little head against my clean muslin sleeve. I gained my end, however, as I knew from a conversation I overheard, just outside the window Fred never seems

to think I use my ears for any other purpose but to hang my ear-rings in, but I can
hear through a stone wall.

" You are very much mistaken, Fred,"
said a voice (it was Seymour's, I knew in
a minute). " She is not so utterly selfish ;
she is reading to Louey now, when I know
she would rather be out playing croquet
with us."

" It isn't out of goodness or love for
Louey, though," said that hateful Fred.
" She has some end of her own, you may be
sure."

" Don't be so ungenerous, Fred," said
Seymour, almost sternly ; and then they
moved so far away that I couldn't hear any
more.

How I do begin to detest Fred ! He seems
to be looking right through me all the time
with his sharp eyes. But I shall be very
careful and make Seymour like me in spite
of him.

July 31. I am never without something to trouble me, and now I have a bigger thorn than usual.

Last Sunday morning, just as I had settled myself in the seat at church, who should I see, sitting in the middle aisle with the Spencers, but Fanny Blythe! I thought about it all the time my head was down (I always put my head down when I first come into church; I think it is very respectable and lady-like); but I could not feel any more resigned about it. The Spencers told me they had a friend coming to see them, but I hadn't the faintest idea it was Fanny. How provoking! I know she has just come to make me trouble. She will take such pleasure in mortifying me, for, of course, she will be constantly alluding to Aunt Jane, and the small way in which I used to live. The Spencers, without a doubt, know all about it already, and how we only kept one little servant. They will laugh when

they see me, of course, for I had given them
to understand that I was always accustomed
to style, never lifting my finger to do anything, but, as you may say, sitting in kid
gloves from morning till night.

It is very hard to bear, and as I sat there
in church, and the choir began to sing so
tenderly, —

> " Gently, Lord, oh gently lead us,
>   Through this lonely vale of tears, — "

I broke right down, and cried very hard.
It was so true that life *was* nothing but
a vale of tears, and I had seen so much
trouble for one so young.

Seymour spoke very kindly to me when
church was out, but I didn't tell him exactly
what was the matter. He has such queer
notions, I have to be always on my guard.
So I only said that I was very lonely, and
missed Aunt Jane, and didn't feel as if I
had many friends.

"You *have* met with great losses, cousin Lotty," said he (he always says "Lotty," and I have concluded not to notice it). "It is very sad for a young girl like you to have neither father nor mother;" and then followed some tiresome "*good* talk," about a great Friend who loved me, and would "comfort me as one whom his mother comforteth."

I knew what was the right thing to say, and so, when he finished, I answered, "Oh, yes, that is my only consolation."

"I am very glad to hear *that*," said he, with his bright smile. "These little troubles here are not much after all, are they, cousin? In such a little while it will all be over, and that dear Elder Brother will wipe away all tears from our eyes." And again there was that strange, sweet look in his face.

I can't help admiring Seymour, and wondering at him too, he is always so happy.

To be sure he has been sufficiently restored to his health to go back to his studies, but he has to be very careful, and is constantly in fear of another attack. Yet he is never depressed or ill-humored, always bright and cheerful, ready to enter into any one's plans. I thought for a moment, as I looked at him that Sunday morning, that I would let everything else go, and try to be good. In fact, I said to cousin Seymour, —

" I feel that the only thing of any importance in this world is to be good and unselfish, and — "

But just then Fred, who overheard me, turned around, making the most horrid face, with big goggle eyes, and made me so angry, I forgot everything else, thinking how I should pay him for his impudence.

He does fairly persecute me; there is no other word for it: and a dreadful thought has just occurred to me, — suppose he and Fanny Blythe should get together! They would be kindred spirits, that's certain; and they'd just make me a mark for all their ridicule and ill-nature. I must try to prevent it. I shall not call on Fanny, nor let Ida go either.

I am getting a little comfort from my book, which I have been writing for the last fortnight. I express myself very handsomely, but I haven't got the plot quite to my satisfaction yet. I am writing the adventures of a selfish, conceited girl, and I will confess to my journal that I have taken Fanny Blythe for my model. I wonder if she will recognize herself when she sees it in print!

To give some idea of my facility of expression, and also what I have to suffer from Fred, I shall record something that happened within the last week.

I had been thinking I would like to give Seymour some idea of my talent in this line, so I wrote out one or two beautiful

thoughts, and dropped them, as if by acci-
dent, in the upper hall, by his room door.

The first was this, written on my birth-
day, July 26.

" Passed, to-day, the fifteenth mile-stone
in my journey of life. Am I on the King's
highway, and how many years to heaven
now ?"

The second idea was very poetical,—
something about each star being a " bright
oasis in the blue desert of the heavens."

I was very much pleased with myself
when these two brilliant thoughts occurred
to me.

Why is it I am so unfortunate ? It was
just my luck that Seymour was gone all
the morning, and my precious paper fell
into the hands of that wretched Fred.

It was tucked under my door again that
same evening, with another paper pinned
to it, with something written in Fred's ugly
boy hand : " If you really wish for infor-

mation, my dear cousin Charlotte Adelaide Patti Rosa Bonheur, I will tell you that you are nowhere near the 'King's highway,' but, according to careful survey, are in a dirty little by-path in the wilderness of Sin. As for the number of years before you reach heaven, I've ciphered all the afternoon; my slate's full of figures, and I'm nowhere near the answer yet. You have studied geometry some, I believe. If you can tell me how soon two diverging lines may be expected to come together, it will help a little on this tough problem.

"P. S. Your poetical thought I've enclosed to Tennyson!"

Mean, contemptible boy! I haven't given him the satisfaction of knowing that I ever found his spiteful paper, but have appeared perfectly unconscious when he made any allusions to the matter. I can see he is disappointed. He would have been so delighted if I had taken it to heart.

But that wasn't such a bad idea, sending that little gem about the stars to Tennyson. I wonder what Fred would say if I should have a letter from the great poet some day, thanking me for the beautiful thought, and urging me to cultivate my talent? It makes me laugh to think how he may have over-reached himself this time.

CHAPTER V.

IS IT I?

AUGUST 6. I have been having such a disagreeable time with that little bother, Loucy. He seems to have the most passionate admiration for beauty, and he comes almost every day, begging that he may lie on my bed a little while, and watch me while I put flowers in my hair or try on my ribbons.

I never let him stay though, unless he first sets my room to rights. Aunt is so absurd about that. There are plenty of servants in the house, but she insists that Ida and I shall take care of our own rooms, and keep them just so neat, and everything folded to a thread in the drawers. Now I

am so busy between my diary and my book,
that I have no time for such little things,
and Ida has grown so disobliging lately
that if I get even half my mending out of
her I think I have done well.

So I generally have Loucy pick up everything he can find on the floor, and dust
the chairs, and every few days put the
drawers in order. By the time that is done
he is so tired, crawling around with his little crooked back, that he doesn't talk much,
but just creeps on the bed, and lies quite
still. That's *one* comfort.

But to-day, after resting a while, he suddenly cried out, —

"What a beautiful, straight back you
have, Cousin Charlotte Adelaide, and how
easy you dance about on your feet! You
must be very glad to be so pretty!"

I knew he was thinking of the great contrast between us, and I patted his little
crooked spine in a pitying way, meaning to

be kind, but he shrank away as if I hurt
him.

"I shall be different some day," said he,
half laughing, half crying. "Seymour says
so, and I read about it too. In the twinkling of an eye I shall be changed. How I
wish the time would come!"

"Don't talk so gloomy, Loucy," I cried,
"or you shall go right away. *I* don't want
the time to come, and I don't want to be
changed either."

"Don't you suppose you *could* be prettier, cousin Charlotte Adelaide?" said
Loucy, very timidly.

"I don't see how I could," said I; and I
don't. I never think of the angels now but
they seem to have my eyes and hair. I
can't imagine anything prettier.

"But what is it about being raised a spiritual body?" said the tiresome child, with
his eyes so big and bright he hardly looked
human.

"I don't know nor care," said I, quite out of patience, "and if you don't talk as other children do, you shan't stay in the room another minute."

So I didn't hear anything more for a long time. Then he said very low, —

" Cousin Charlotte Adelaide, would ' other children ' talk about pic-nics ? "

" That's a little better," said I.

" Well, then, there's going to be a great pic-nic to-morrow, and we're all going ! "

" Not you, I hope, Humpy Dumpy ! " Loucy began to cry.

" This is a little too much ! " said I, feeling quite nervous with his fretful ways. " Go right off to your own room; I only want pleasant, cheerful boys around me ; " and I sent him away sobbing like a baby as he is.

Then I went to find Ida, who says it is really so, and that we are all invited.

How splendid it will be ! The only drawback is, that Fanny Blythe is invited, and in some way I'm sure her envy and ill-nature will spoil the day for me. However, I won't cross that bridge before I come to it. I shall be very dignified with Fanny, and put her down if she makes any allusion to the past. I shall pretend not to understand what she is talking about.

By the way, when I contrast my old humble life with my present splendor, I can't help believing that I'm a kind of favorite of fortune, and that whenever I need anything, specially, it will be brought to me.

For instance, Aunt Jane did very well for my baby days, but as soon as my beauty, talents, and increasing years, called for a more exalted station, Uncle Willoughby seems to have been providentially raised up to place me in it.

I feel confident some splendid fate is in store for me, and I should think those around me would see it, and not be always calling upon me and expecting me to spend my time in trifles.

Aug. 6. P. M. Seymour has not been quite so kind to me these last few days, and I have often caught him looking at me in a queer sort of a way, as if he were thinking about me and studying me. I don't like it at all; and this afternoon, especially, he has made me very uncomfortable.

About an hour ago I went down to sit on the piazza with my book, and there was Seymour with Louey on his lap.

The baby had been crying, and I'm afraid telling something, for he grew very red when he saw me, and Seymour looked at me with a sad sort of a smile. However, he didn't say anything,— that is, not to me. He was telling Louey little simple stories, too simple to repeat, and yet they made me uneasy.

"Now, I'll tell you a story about a conceited goose," said Seymour.

" Yes, *do*," said that foolish Louey.

" A goose, who lived in a barn-yard, one morning remarked to her sisters, ' It seems to me that we are the most important creatures in the world. The horse is bigger, but he has to work; the oxen have to plow; the cow is kept just to give milk; but *we* live like queens, and do nothing. There is *man*, too, — quite a superior animal, I should think, only he looks wretchedly in the water, — but he seems to have been created simply to mix our food, and bring it to our very mouths, and make us comfortable generally.

" How he must admire and envy us, we are so very graceful and accomplished; we swim as well as we can walk. How superior we are, too, in the elegance of our garments, to which we never have to give a thought. When man is tired he must take off his nice coat before he can rest himself; but we sleep all night in our snowy feath-

ers, and are ready to make calls at sunrise,
without spot or wrinkle. Then we have no
cares of housekeeping, or thinking where
we shall get our next meal. Man was created to be our slave, and relieve us of everything burdensome or disagreeable. We
are certainly greatly distinguished and fa-
vored, and I feel that some glorious fate is
in store for us, especially for *me*, who am
the fattest and handsomest goose of you
all !'

" But that night, that very goose had her
neck chopped, and was served up with ap-
ple-sauce the next day."

Louey laughed loud in his childish, shal-
low way, but I wouldn't lift my eyes.

" Well, if you like that I'll tell you another about a selfish fly," said Seymour.

" There was once a fly who had very
pretty wings, all rainbow and gold, and be-
lieved she was very superior to her brothers
and sisters. This fly always gobbled up

anything nice she came across, without
ever telling any one else. She chose the
best places on the mirror and chandelier,
and grew more disobliging every day of her
life.

" One day a very small fly, that could just
walk alone, crept up to her, and asked very
humbly,—

" ' Will you please show me the way to the
sugar-bowl ? I'm dying with hunger.'

" ' Not I,' said the selfish fly. ' My time
is too important for that ; I can't waste my
strength in such trifles ; I've a great work
before me.'

" ' What, pray ? ' said the little fly.

" ' Tiresome creature,' she replied. ' Did
you ever see those shining specks up above
us,. which men call stars ? '

" ' I saw them for the first time last night,'
said the little fly, in a weak voice, ' and
some one said they were big worlds, bigger
than this.'

"'Nonsense,' said the other, impatiently. 'I will tell you a secret. There is a race of flies with golden wings like mine, who are destined to be very famous. They stay here a while to grow handsomer and grander, and when they are strong enough they fly away up there, to be greatly honored for ever. Those stars, as men call them, are only golden flies crawling on the blue wall of heaven.'

"That night the proud fly concluded she was strong enough for her trip. She set out triumphantly, and had almost reached the eaves of the house, when she tripped in a spider's web, was all tangled and helpless in a minute, and, alas! was gobbled up long before morning!

"The moral is, my dear Louey, that when we think of ourselves more highly than we ought to think, we are not a whit wiser than the goose or silly fly. And just as we hope we are about to realize our brilliant dreams, we are pretty sure to have a cruel disappointment."

I was pretty sure of another thing too, and that was, that Seymour was telling these silly little stories for *me*, instead of Loucy. It made me very angry, and when he began again,—

"There was once a cat who was so fond of dress that she wouldn't lay off her furs even in the warmest summer weather,—" I just picked up my book and ran.

It is so strange! Every one in the house seems to think I am conceited and selfish, though I'm sure I don't see why. It is true I have beauty and talent enough to make almost any girl in the world vain, but the only wonder is that I don't think more of myself.

CHAPTER VI.

AUG. 8. Well, the pic-nic is over, and I don't believe there was one there who didn't have a better time than I.

In the first place, every one seemed to take such a fancy to Fanny Blythe. It was perfectly unaccountable, and very provoking. She isn't in the least pretty, and as I stood by Seymour in the grove, I could not keep from making fun of her turn-up nose.

Instead of laughing with me, Seymour only looked very grave. " Did you ever hear," said he, " that ridiculing others is only an oblique way of praising ourselves?"

This was very disagreeable, especially as

153

I could not help confessing to myself that I had hoped to draw Seymour's attention to my own nose, which is a beautiful Grecian.

" You can't say she is pretty, any way," said I, shortly.

" I think she has the very best kind of beauty," said he. " She has a remarkably bright, intelligent face, and, better than all, I can read from her eyes and pleasant mouth that she is kind-hearted and self-sacrificing. I should like to know her."

I longed to tell him how he was mistaken, but felt sure I should be misunderstood, and so stood trying to smile, while everybody crowded around Fanny and made her of the greatest importance.

In the very beginning of the day it was proposed that some one should be queen, and decide on all the games, and tell us all what to do.

I thought it was an excellent plan, for I was almost sure they would choose me. I helped them make a very pretty wreath, for I have a great deal of taste, and then just stood smiling, trying to look unconscious till they should come to crown me.

To my great surprise and mortification, they never seemed to give me a thought, but passed right by, and crowned Fanny Blythe!

How dreadful it was! No one knows how hard it was for me to bow down with the rest, as they all vowed allegiance to their queen. I almost bit my tongue in two trying to control myself, and as soon as I thought I would not be noticed I stole away into the thickest part of the wood to have a good cry.

But I couldn't have even that comfort in peace. All of a sudden some one touched my hand, and I looked up, hoping it was Seymour, coming to comfort me, and tell me they had made a great mistake. But no! it was only that bother!

"Cousin Charlotte Adelaide," panted the wretched, little, piping voice, "it was too bad not to make you the queen" (the little crooked mite *pitied* me!) "But *I* have made you a wreath, and will be your most faithful subject;" and he tried to put a little snarl of daisies on my head.

For once in my life I was out of patience, and just boxed his ears, and tore off the mean little flowers and stamped them under my feet.

Loucy looked at me a moment perfectly wild, then gave one great sob, and threw himself down with his face to the ground.

I was sorry the minute I did it; for, as ill-luck would have it, Seymour, who had been looking for Loucy, just came through the trees, and saw it all.

"Cruel!" said he, looking at me in a way which makes my cheeks burn even to remember it. "Take heed how ye offend one of these little ones!" and lifting Loucy very tenderly in his arms, he kissed him, and carried him away.

How sweet it must be to be loved! Nobody loves me. At that moment I believe I would rather have been little, crooked Loucy, than the beautiful Charlotte Adelaide Peacock.

Of course I didn't enjoy myself much the rest of the day. I cried a while over my troubles after Seymour left me, and thought how unfortunate I was; a poor, friendless orphan, with everybody trying their best to make me unhappy. At last, as nobody seemed to think of coming to find me, I strolled slowly back. There they were, swinging, romping, and playing games; nobody seemed to miss me, or care what had become of me.

What struck me as particularly disagreeable, was, that Fanny Blythe was sitting between Fred and Loucy, evidently trying her best to be entertaining. Loucy was talking very fast too, and it made my heart beat to think what his simple little tongue might tell about me. He's such a little sieve, if he thinks anybody likes him; and I knew Fanny was just the one to flatter him, and draw him out.

I found I was not mistaken: a little later in the day, when, rambling in the wood, all alone, of course, I slipped and fell down a great precipice. I screamed with pain, and every one ran.

"Pshaw!" said that heartless Fred, jumping down beside me. "You're not hurt a bit; it's no more than falling off a chair."

"I'm hurt terribly!" I cried; "if the pain is one bit harder I shall die!" and I screamed again.

Then Fanny Blythe bent over, and whispered,—"let the fox tear out his heart, and never complained."

I screamed louder than ever then. I was so angry I would like to have knocked her

down. All I could do by way of revenge
was to make a grand fuss, and say that my
foot was so badly sprained that I must be
carried home immediately. I was of some
consequence at last, for I broke up the
games, and kept them all waiting on me.
Some of the boys had to go for a wagon,
and the girls ran to a farmhouse for cam-
phor and vinegar, and altogether it took up
so much time that they all concluded to
break up and go home when I did. That
was some comfort, — to break up their hateful old pic-nic.

Louey didn't dare to come near me when
I was hurt; but I saw the tears in his baby
eyes, and he made Fanny take his handkerchief to bind up my foot. He hasn't a grain
of spirit.

To tell the truth, my foot is hardly hurt
at all; but I have to keep up appearances,
and stay in my room, and let Ann bandage
it up in vinegar.

CHAPTER VII.

THE MORE EXCELLENT WAY.

AUG. 10. It is very tiresome to be playing sick this beautiful morning, while they are all out at croquet. No one comes near me any more, not even Loucy, who seems afraid of me. I am just as lonely and forlorn as I can be.

I have been trying to write a little in my book, but somehow it won't grow interesting, and I have almost decided to give it up. What does it matter, after all, if I lay by this talent for the present with the others? I may become just as famous by my beauty as if I wore myself out writing books or painting pictures. Perhaps, after all, that is exactly what I was made for,—

just to be beautiful, — a lily of the field, that toils not, neither does it spin, and yet Solomon in all his glory isn't to be compared to one of *us.*

I am wonderfully beautiful, — there is no denying it. What if I am not as useful as some others! A lily is a great deal better liked than a bed of catnip or a root of rhubarb. Now, it always seems to me that Ida, working around in her quiet way, good to amuse the babies and keep them still, is just like catnip; and Fanny Blythe, who is clever certainly, but so intensely disagreeable, is rhubarb. Who wouldn't be the lily?

I am going to lie on the bed a while, and look at myself in my little hand-glass.

Evening. Such a horrid talk as I have had with Seymour! I was lying on the bed, looking at myself, and feeling in the most pleasant, amiable state of mind, for my skin was like satin, and wasn't the least

11

freckled nor tanned after the pic-nic, and it seemed as if my eyes grew larger, and the eyelashes longer, every day. It was very provoking to be interrupted by a knock at the door, though, to be sure, I was better pleased to see Seymour coming in than any of the rest of the family. I slipped the little glass under the quilt, and tried to look as if I were very patient under my sufferings. I know he thought I was pretty, lying there in my white wrapper, for I saw it in his eyes, though he tried to look very hard and grave, while he asked me very coldly if I " felt any better."

I didn't like his manner at all, and so I said,—

" It can't be of any interest to you, or any one else, how I feel. I haven't a friend in the world."

He didn't contradict me, as one would have expected, of course, but just asked, in his quiet way,—

" Do you know what is the reason ? "

That was a little too much, and I burst out crying and sobbing with all my might. It has always been a comfort to me that I look prettier than ever when I cry, — like a rose wet in a shower. My face never gets swollen and red as Fanny Blythe's does.

I might have spared myself all that extra exertion, though, for that cold-blooded Seymour didn't make the slightest effort to console me. In fact, I think he looked out of the window till I stopped from sheer exhaustion, and then said, in his ordinary way, —

" I am going away on a little sea-voyage, for my health, cousin. I shall start to-morrow, and probably be gone all the vacation. You will excuse me for troubling you in your room; but you do not come down stairs now, and I did not like to go away without seeing you once more."

"Thank you," said I, very stiffly.

"And, cousin," said he, his mouth trembling a little, " I can not feel easy unless I say something before I go. I am afraid you will think it is hard and cruel, but it is only because I truly love you."

I felt as if something dreadful was coming, and was too frightened to say a word.

" You told me when I first came," continued he, " that you were a Christian, and I hoped it was so; but, cousin, you must not deceive yourself; you know nothing about it. What is it to be a Christian ? First, of course, to love God with heart, soul, and strength; and secondly (and the command is just as binding), to love your fellow-men, your neighbor, as yourself."

"And how do you know I do not, Mr. Importance ? " said I.

He flushed a little. " Forgive me, cousin, but you love only one person in all the world, and that is your beautiful self."

" Prove it ! " said I, just choking.

" Well, then, think over your cousins, your friends, your neighbors; if you do not actually dislike and despise them, you are at least indifferent to them. Their plans, wishes, hopes, are of no importance to you. You would not turn over your hand to oblige them. Then I have noticed — I must tell you the truth, cousin — that you are very haughty and hard-hearted with the poor. Poor Mrs. Bingham is as much your neighbor as rich Miss Spencer, and yet you swept proudly by, and made no offer to help her, when you met her staggering in the lane a few days ago, having grown faint in the sunshine with her heavy load. Then how you mortified her son John, the day of the pic-nic. When he made his humble admiring bow, you returned it with a rude, haughty stare, as much as to say, 'How can that fellow have the impudence to bow to the elegant Miss Peacock?' And yet John and his mother are

devoted, consistent Christians. If you are
one also, as you hope, they have the very
highest claim upon you. God has made
you all of one family,—you are all his children."

"And yet I suppose one may be allowed
to choose associates who are congenial even
among God's children," said I, with proper
spirit.

"Yes, to be sure, we may certainly make
our selections, and choose whom we please
for our intimate friends, but we have no
excuse for treating any one with contempt
and unkindness, no matter how inferior he
may appear.

"You would not treat a *king* as you did
John, but how do you know what God has
in store for him? It doth not yet appear
what he shall be.

"When you meet God's children, remember they are 'kings and priests to

God' yet to be. Be very careful you do not make some great mistake."

Seymour gets up such queer ideas, I couldn't think for a moment what to say; so he went on : —

"You are very pretty, cousin, but God looks on the heart. Fanny Blythe, quick-tongued, but genuinely conscientious and self-sacrificing ; little crooked, cheerful Loucy, waiting patiently to be changed, — are fairer in God's sight than you."

"Cruel!" sobbed I, in earnest this time. "How dare you talk so to me!"

Seymour wiped his eyes. He pretended it pained him to tell me this, but I know he enjoyed it. Everybody likes to torture me. In a moment he was at it again.

"You have told me you hoped to be famous some day, and perhaps you have talents —"

"Perhaps, indeed!" said I, scornfully.

"Yes, it is by no means certain," said

he, in that quiet, detestable way of his.
"You are very conceited, cousin; if you
had been humbler you would not have had
so many mortifications. He that is down
need fear no fall. God resisteth the proud,
and giveth grace to the humble."

"Proud, conceited, selfish!" I sobbed;
"have you any more pleasant things to
say?"

"Only this," said he: "as I said before,
you are longing to be famous, and I will not
deny that earthly honor and admiration is
exceedingly pleasant. If we were to live
here always I should bend every energy to
its attainment. But the change must come
so soon. In that hour when our clinging
hands must loose their hold of life, when
we lie helplessly floating between two
worlds, what will comfort us most,—to know
that we stand high on the earthly roll of
fame,—a Jenny Lind, a Rosa Bonheur, a
Tennyson,—or that our names are not un-

known in that great land whither we are
going?—that the Master knows that we,
that you, have followed him, have gone
about doing good; that the sum of human
miscry is less for your having lived; that
your name is written in the book of life,
with this most precious record concerning
you, ' She hath done what she could'? Oh,
what happiness, what never-ending fame,
were this!' "

He paused a moment to steady his voice.
"Is it not better to lead this grand, useful
life, than just to be seeking your own pet-
ty advancement? Think what it must be to
hear, always making music in your heart,
' Inasmuch as ye have done it unto the
least of these ye have done it unto me!'
A kindness done to the least, the meanest,
of those He came to save,—He will take
it as a personal favor. In the humble
thanks you shall hear Christ's voice,—' You
have done it unto *me!*' What a wonderful

honor! We, so weak, so inferior, may do the
Saviour a kindness. Cousin, promise me
you will think of it."

I covered my face, and wouldn't answer.
He had been such a bore!

He waited a few minutes.

" Have you nothing to say before I go ?"

" If you *will* make me speak," said I, " I
don't think you have any right to preach
sermons before you are licensed, and I wish
you'd go away now, for I'm tired, and want
to sleep."

He gave a long, long sigh, and saying,
" Good-by, then, cousin," stooped to kiss
me; but I pushed him away. To think of
pretending affection after insulting me so
cruelly!

Ida came to my room a little while afterwards to tell me that odious Fanny Blythe
was here to tea, and to ask me if I couldn't
come down. But I was too unhappy.

" Seymour has been proving to me that I

am not a fit companion for such excellence,"
said I; " she must excuse me."

Later in the evening, I heard them all
out on the piazza, singing and telling stories. How happy they were!

At last Fanny was going home, and Seymour was going with her. What a pleasant walk she would have through the fields,
while I sat crying in my dark room!

"I am sorry not to have seen Lotty,"
said the hypocrite, as she tied her hat.

"What have you done to her, Seymour?"
laughed Fred. "You might as well have
let her alone. I should think you'd have
found out by this time there is no use in
wasting the 'good seed' in that quarter."

"We shall see," said Seymour, cheerfully.
"It isn't everything best that blossoms the
same summer you plant it!"

I heard every word in the still summer
night. How cruel and heartless to talk me

over in such a public way! I shall never forgive them.

Oh dear! I'm tired of my life, and I'm tired of this journal! Such a record of mortifications, I can't bear the sight of it. I believe I won't write in it any more.

CHAPTER VIII.

THE COMING FEAST.

EC. 15. While stirring up my drawer this morning, to find my stockings, which some way always get mixed up with my collars and ribbons, I stumbled across my old diary, and have taken a notion to write in it once more.

How disagreeably it did leave off, and how very angry I was with Seymour! I couldn't get that sermon out of my head for a long time, and once in a while I used to try to be more obliging, but it was a great bother, and I've forgotten almost all about it now, thank fortune!

I haven't had a very pleasant fall and winter, aunt's family have grown so cold

and unsympathetic. I spend a great deal
of time in my room, and only come down
when there are visitors; strangers always
admire me greatly, and I have to make that
console me in my lonely hours.

We are to have a very large party here
on Christmas, and among them will be Mr.
Barnard, who insists upon taking my portrait. He will stay a few days and begin it
here. I expect to enjoy myself exceedingly.

I have been out all the morning, seeing
about some natural flowers, which of course
are difficult to obtain at this season. I
overheard Fred telling Ida that Mrs. Bingham had some splendid scarlet geraniums,
and a few other flowers, which he could get
for her to put in her hair, Christmas.

I thought it was very selfish in them not
to think of me, when they knew I was going to leave off black at the holidays, and
should particularly need flowers when my
portrait was taken. So I just slipped on

my hat and cloak, and ran down to Mrs.
Bingham's myself. Fred will never know
but what it was my own idea, for I was in
the back parlor when he spoke of it, and
slipped out before he saw me.

Sure enough, Mrs. Bingham's small windows were crowded with flowers. How
they grow so finely in that little poverty-
stricken hole, I don't know, but there they
were, and I told her I had come to engage
every bud and blossom that would be out
on Christmas day.

Mrs. Bingham always is very unfriendly
with me, for some reason, but to-day she
was positively rude. She only held her
door open on a little crack, so that I really
had quite a squeeze getting in. I am sure
I didn't stay a minute longer than I could
help in her room, for it had a very disagreeable odor; but it had occurred to me that
my white dress would be lovely trimmed
with wreaths of greens, and I wanted John
to go to the woods and bring me some.

The lazy, unmannerly fellow was lying full length on a rude lounge at the farther side of the room, and didn't stir as I approached him.

"Don't wake him, please, Miss," said Mrs. Bingham; "he isn't well at all."

Mothers are all alike; the idea of making a baby of that great, strong John!

"But I must speak to him a minute," said I, giving his arm a shake; "John, wake up!"

He started up, very red and wild, saying queer, jumbled words, while his ill-mannered mother just pushed me right out of the room.

"I wouldn't have had him wakened for a kingdom, Miss," said she, putting up her apron; and I ran home, for I hate scenes. Why is it that I am always stumbling upon something unpleasant?

But I shall have a splendid time Christmas!

CHAPTER IX.

THE LOWEST ROOM.

MAY 10. For the first time in months I have been allowed to use my eyes more than a few minutes at a time, and I have chosen to write a while in my diary. It seems right that this record of my folly and selfishness should be completed with the history of my bitter punishment. I shall continue my story from where I left it just before the Christmas, which was to have been so brilliant and triumphant.

I remember, after coming home from Mrs. Bingham's cottage, I spent the rest of the day, and several days following, arranging my dress for the great party; only going

out to spend my little allowance for ribbons
and trumpery for my own adornment.

The children were all happy and eager,
preparing little surprises for each other, but
I couldn't spare anything from myself, even
to buy a toy for the baby.

All the time, patient, forgiving Loucy
was carving me a bracelet out of different
kinds of wood. Ida was working my name
on a pretty embroidered handkerchief, and
Fred had bought me Jean Ingelow's Poems
in green and gold.

I felt very much ashamed on Christmas
morning when I had nothing to give them
in return, and I think they saw it, for I remember they said kindly,—

"Never mind, cousin; you didn't know it
was our custom: another Christmas you
will think of it."

I was in terror lest they should find out
how selfish I had been about the flowers,
but Fred, who went after them for Ida, only

said that John was very sick, and the neighbors advised him not to go to the house, for there was a rumor that it was some dreadful and contagious disease, although his mother kept very still about it.

This worried me greatly, especially as I had a terrible head-ache, which seemed to grow worse every minute.

As the day advanced I had to lie down, although I heard the gay company arriving, and Mr. Barnard asking for me. I shall be better by evening, I thought, but when at last the gas was lighted, and, exerting my strong will, I rose and tried to dress, I staggered and fell, before the first curl was brushed round my finger. Again and again did I try, and fail, before I could give up all idea of the brilliant parlors and Christmas tree, and lie in my little room instead, groaning and crying with pain.

I remember listening for a while, with a bitter, rebellious heart, to the music, the laughing and shouting. Then everything becomes confused. I seemed drifting away into a horrible, blank space, stretching my hands in vain to Fred and Fanny Blythe, who were far away, safe on a bright cloud above me.

"Save me! save me!" I cried.

But they only laughed, and I thought I heard them say to each other,—"let it tear out his heart, and didn't complain. Now is a good time to learn self-control."

Swift as light the scene changed. There was a terrible rushing noise, and I was in a little boat on the maddest water just at the edge of a frightful fall. I stood up and screamed wildly. No help! Over we went, down, down,—and then, thank God, I did not know any more.

It might have been the next minute, or it might have been ages after, that I opened my eyes, and found myself in my bed in my own room. The pain was all gone;

only a stray lock of hair on my forehead troubled me, and when I wanted to brush it off, my hand lay like a log at my side. Neither could I turn myself in bed, although, from some slight noise, I was quite conscious some one else was in the room, and I wished greatly to see if it were Ida or Loucy.

At last, with quite an effort, I managed to make a slight noise, and immediately an old woman, whom I had never seen before, was bending over me.

" Ah, you are better, poor child! you will live, thank God ! "

" Who are you ? " said I, shortly, for I didn't like the idea of strangers being so free in my room.

" Hush, my dear ! " said she ; " you have been very sick, and I mustn't talk to you now."

Then away she bustled for some gruel, which I had to take whether I would or no.

In fact, I was so weak, she had everything her own way, and I minded her like a baby.

A day or two passed, and I grew stronger under her care. She was a kindly old woman, and would turn me a dozen times that I might keep her in sight, while she set the room in order, or warmed my light dinner. The idea came in my foolish head that she was like a dried-up old fairy ministering to a beautiful princess. In fact, I told her so, one day, when I was provoked with some of her tyrannical ways.

She only said, "Poor child! poor child!" and actually wiped a tear from her eyes.

I could not understand such an excess of pity. What did it mean, when I was getting better and stronger every day? It irritated me greatly, and I wouldn't speak to the good old woman for half a day.

In the mean time I began to think it very strange that my aunt and cousins had not been in to see me.

" Where are they all ? " I asked the nurse.

" Gone to Philadelphia to visit your uncle's sister."

" Gone to enjoy themselves, while I was so very ill ! " said I, bitterly.

" It was thought best they should go," said the old nurse. " Some day you will know the reason why."

This set me to thinking again. Why did the old woman look so pityingly at me ? What terrible thing was hanging over me ? But I could not find out, and the slow days passed by without any variation, till one morning, when I was washed very carefully and dressed clean from top to toe, and James and Ann came to carry me into another room.

" What is this for ? " I asked.

" To give you a little change," said nurse, pleasantly. " You must be very tired of seeing those same four walls. Besides, your room is to be cleaned before your aunt and cousins come back."

"I don't see why," said I, petulantly. "You kept it as neat as a pin."

Turning suddenly, for I could move now, I caught Ann with her hands up, making gestures to James.

"Well, Ann, are you going crazy? What is the matter? Am I so changed?"

"You are very thin, Miss," said Ann, and hurried away, pretending some one called her.

"Well, don't act as if I were a hobgoblin," said I; "my cheeks will be full again before long."

Then, being very tired and weak, I fell asleep, and didn't think anything more of the vexatious subject till the next day. Then, as the old nurse was reading aloud a chapter from the Bible, as she always would, without asking my permission, she came to this verse: —

"Favor is deceitful, and beauty is vain, but a woman that feareth the Lord, she shall be praised."

I never liked that verse much, but she read it twice over, and looked at me over her spectacles to see if I heard.

"It is well enough for you to comfort yourself with that verse," I thought, "for you are as ugly as a toad, but I—" and then I thought I would like to look at myself once more. I had spoken of it two or three times before, but she had always put me off with some excuse, and now she jumped up, saying,—

"Oh! I hear a carriage; your aunt has come."

And I was left alone by myself.

In about half an hour, just as I was trying in my willfulness to totter across the room to the dressing bureau, my cousins came trooping in. They all kissed me, were so glad I was better, and wanted me

to look at the pretty presents they had
brought me from the city.

But my suspicions were aroused, and I
watched them all very narrowly. It seemed
to me they were all constrained, and little
Louey kept his eyes fixed on me, with his
face very red, looking as if he was going to
cry.

" Bring me a glass! " cried I, excitedly,
to the nurse. " I *will* have one. I shall get
it myself, if you won't! "

" Bring it," said aunt, in a low voice.
" There must be a first time."

Nurse brought it. I seized it eagerly.
Oh, frightful! my beautiful face was red
and scarred; my pretty hair gone, shorn
close to my head!

" Oh! it can not be! It is a horrible
dream! Aunt, Ida, tell me; I am not hid-
eous! It is not I! " and in my rage and
despair I brought my clenched fist down

on the faithful mirror, shivering it into a thousand pieces.

Ida was sobbing aloud, Fred stole out of the room, and Loucy sank upon his knees.

" O Jesus," he sobbed, " comfort cousin Charlotte Adelaide, and tell her if we're patient and good you'll make us beautiful some day."

" *We!* " " *Us!* " I screamed. " Yes, you are quite right, Loucy. I belong to *your* company now."

Loucy did not seem to hear, but aunt's face flushed. " I do not know about that," said she, lifting his slight figure tenderly.

" Oh, how am I ever to bear it! It is too horrible! I *will not* have it so! " I cried, in impotent rage.

" We will all love you more than ever, cousin Charlotte Adelaide," said the poor little boy, tears streaming down his thin cheeks.

" *Never* call me that name again! " I

shrieked. "There is no Charlotte Adelaide; she is dead, gone for ever! Oh, how I wish she *were* dead! But this *will* kill me. Go, let me die in peace!"

Aunt drew away the children, and I was left alone,— alone to sob and mourn incessantly, and to stop my ears when nurse tried to comfort me.

Towards evening Ann came up to let nurse go down to tea. I called her to the bed.

"Ann, what was the matter with John Bingham?"

"Small-pox, Miss."

"And I had it too?" I groaned.

"Yes, Miss."

"But I was vaccinated?"

"Not since you were a baby, and it run out they said. But, Miss, don't take on so. There was every care taken of you. There was wet cloths on your poor face all the time, that it shouldn't be marked, and it

isn't but very little. If you could see
John's now! Besides, Miss, the red will
leave your face little by little; you'll look
quite yourself again in a year's time, — maybe less."

"In a year's time!" I said, bursting out
afresh. And so I mourned day after day,
refusing to be comforted, until I had wea-
ried the patience of every one in the house.

"Sin no more," said nurse one day, "lest
a worse evil befall you."

"What *can* be worse?" I cried, in my
wickedness and rebellion. But my question
was answered.

Incessant weeping and mourning, with
refusal to take any food, threw me into a
low fever, accompanied by acute inflamma-
tion of the eyes.

At first, when I knew that I was again
dangerously ill, I only felt a kind of triumph. I imagined I had not had sufficient
sympathy; they hadn't the faintest idea of

my misery. They didn't believe me when I said it would kill me, but they should see I was right.

But this state of mind did not last long; I roused one day from a sort of stupor to the consciousness that several persons were kneeling around my bed. What were they doing?

Was that my cold aunt, pleading so tenderly that I might have one more chance to lead a nobler and better life, to the glory of God's holy name? Was that my little Louey, speaking to his dear friend Jesus in behalf of " cousin Charlotte Adelaide"? And the old nurse, too, putting up her strong, homely petitions for the same unworthy person?

I could not see, for the room was perfectly dark on account of my sensitive eyes, but I heard only too well.

So it was really possible, perhaps even *certain*, that I must die!

It was a most overwhelming thought! I could not stir nor speak, even when they softly kissed me, and Loucy, patting my cheek, sobbed with angelic pity, —

"Poor, poor cousin Charlotte Adelaide!"

They all went out on tiptoe, and left me in silence and darkness; but I could not sleep again; a perfect whirlwind of thought was sweeping through my brain.

To die so young, so unprepared! Oh, it was horrible! I *must* live, live any way; disfigured, deformed, it was no matter, so only that I might still cling to life, — sweet life! I had no hope beyond.

Why hadn't they stayed and prayed longer for me, — they who knew God as a friend? Why didn't they think what it was to lie down in the dark, cold grave, as I must soon, and be no more seen? I didn't dare pray for myself, after forgetting God so many years.

"Ida! Loucy!" I called faintly, and then

almost unconsciously the cry broke from me,—" Jesus, thou Son of David, have mercy on me!"

It was the cry of the blind man by the wayside, and even as his petition was heard, so the scales seemed to fall from my inner sight, and my soul's eyes were opened.

My past life was all before me in a new light. I saw my patient, loving Aunt Jane admiring me as a superior being, sacrificing her comfort to my slightest whim, while I, ungrateful, received her service only as the homage due me, and let her spend her feeble strength, till Death, more pitiful, gave her the rest I begrudged her.

I saw large-souled, sensible Fanny Blythe, laughing at my foibles, but ready to be the truest friend, while I insulted and repelled her with charges of envy and pride, which had their dwelling only in my own heart.

I saw patient little Loucy,—with every claim upon my tenderest compassion,—

broken-hearted, under my selfishness and cruelty.

There was nothing to relieve the picture; Seymour had told but half the truth. Utter selfishness, haughtiness, and vanity! Aunt Willoughby, Ida, Fred, Mrs. Bingham, John,—all the world were witnesses against me.

How had I always sought for the chief places at every feast, and now behold me sent with shame to take the lowest room,—the lowest room!

In my distress I groaned aloud; nurse was at my side in a minute.

. "Shall I move you, dear, or change your pillows?"

How could she think of such trifles in this dreadful moment?

"I am going to die, nurse!" I gasped. "What will become of me? I am afraid to die!"

She took my hand and kissed me ten-

13

derly. "Behold the Lamb of God, **who** taketh away the sins of the world!"

"How can I?" I cried eagerly.

"Believe on him, trust in him, throw yourself on his mercy, ask him to wash all your sins away in his blood. He will hear you, my dear. He never turned any away."

I wanted to talk more, but nurse was frightened to see me so excited, and forbade it. She brought me a sleeping potion, but I would not take it. I did not dare to waste a moment of the precious time that might be so short.

He who knows the secrets of all hearts alone can tell the misery and struggle of that night; but at last, towards morning, exhausted and almost despairing, I crept to the foot of the cross with my burden of sin and sorrow. I felt keenly what an unworthy offering I was bringing,—a poor, wasted, feeble wreck; but if God only would restore me, I would consecrate to him all I had left,—my youth and the strength he should give me.

After that I grew calmer, and fell into a peaceful sleep, which lasted far into the next day, the holy Sabbath.

" You have had a fine sleep," said nurse, bending over me with her spoon. " Keep up good heart, and all will go well yet. You may be up in a fortnight."

I smiled, and gave silent thanks for this proof that my prayers had been heard.

But my foolish vanity was not dead yet. With the hope of life came many sadder thoughts : a shrinking from the time when I should leave my room, so terribly changed, and perhaps should meet with pity and neglect where I had been so much admired. Mr. Barnard would not want to paint me now !

It was strange that these thoughts must come to trouble the sweet peace and happi ness of my new hope, but they returned again and again.

Towards evening, in the Sabbath twilight, the children were singing, as is their custom.

"Open the door wide, nurse," I said; "I want to hear the words;" and, floating up on Ida's clear voice, I heard distinctly,—

> "Jesus, I my cross have taken,
>   All to leave and follow thee;
>   Naked, poor, despised, forsaken,
>   Thou from hence my all shalt be.
>   Let the world neglect and leave me,
>   They have left my Saviour too;
>   Human hopes have oft deceived me;
>   Thou art faithful, thou art true."

I smiled through my happy tears. Was that Saviour mine, and should anything have power to trouble me?

Ida sang on,—

> "Perish earthly fame and treasure,
>   Come disaster, scorn, and pain;
>   In thy service pain is pleasure;
>   With thy favor, loss is gain."

Yes, I thought, what are my troubles, my loss of beauty, the fading of my earthly dreams of fame, compared to this great gain? Praise the Lord, O my soul, and all that is within me, bless his holy name!

After that day I rapidly improved, and should have soon been out of my room were it not for the trouble with my eyes. Light was exceedingly painful to them, and for a long time we feared they were hopelessly affected. But my kind uncle has spared no expense. I have had the most skillful treatment, and now this sweet, spring morning I can see as well as ever.

My heart is overflowing with gratitude, and I hope my new life will prove it.

Aug. 18. I have been almost too busy to think of my journal this happy summer, the happiest of my life; but this morning I have something to write.

Dear little Loucy, who follows me about, and would wait on me like a slave if I would let him, came to me yesterday, and said, —

" Do you know you are growing my own pretty cousin again ? "

How foolish I am ! The color rushed to my face, and I ran up stairs to take a long look at myself, the first since that unhappy day when I broke the mirror.

I was surprised to find he was half right. My complexion was clearing, the muddy red was almost gone, and my hair had come on in short, bright, wavy curls. There were only two or three pits on my face to remind me for ever of my hard lesson.

At first, I must confess, I was greatly pleased, and then I was frightened. I ran down to find Seymour, who is with us again, and was sitting on his favorite piazza in the sunset.

" Seymour," cried I, all out of breath, " I am growing pretty again ! "

"Yes," said he, smiling; "almost as pretty as ever."

"But I don't want to be 'Charlotte Adelaide' again."

"I don't see any necessity for that," and he smiled still more. "Beauty needn't be a curse. It is a gift from God, to be received with thankfulness, and used for his glory."

"How?" said I.

"A pleasant face is always welcome. Your beauty may make the cause you profess more attractive to a great many, make them more ready to listen to you. You will have a larger influence. Thank God for it."

And I did, very humbly.

"Seymour," said I, after a pause, "I think I have wonderful blessings. I can not understand it. I thought once I never could be forgiven for such great vanity and presumption. Only think how determined I have been to have the first places at every feast, and thought them only my right! Do you think God can really love me? Did you ever know such unbounded selfishness before?"

Seymour smiled brightly. "I remember some one who came with his mother and brother asking Jesus for the first places in heaven,—that one should sit on his right, and the other on his left, when he came into his kingdom."

"And that was—"

"John, the beloved disciple. Jesus loves us through everything," said my kindest cousin.

I wiped away the happy tears.

"But, Seymour, you haven't the least idea how wicked I've been. If you could only see my diary!"

Seymour lifted his hands in comical deprecation.

"What are you two talking about?"

said Fred, coming toward us. " You haven't been writing that book, have you, Lotty ? "

I blushed a little. " I suppose you mean my book about the selfish, conceited girl. No; I gave that up long ago. I was only speaking of my diary."

" Are you quite sure you gave that book up ? " laughed Fred. " What is the diary about ? "

" For shame, Fred ! " cried Seymour.

" No," said I, forcing myself to look up, though my face was all aflame. " Fred is right. I have written my book about that vainest, most selfish girl in the world ; I was writing it all the time, though I didn't know it, and the heroine, instead of Fanny Blythe, was Charlotte Adelaide Peacock ! "

COW-GATE.

203

COW-GATE.

---o---

CHAPTER I.

THE PINK APRON.

"I DECLARE, if she hasn't been washing it," cried Sandy Dunbar, "and hung it right out on the frame!"

Now Sandy, at the time of the exclamation, was carelessly balanced on the sill of an attic window, half in and half out; and as this story is likely to have a good many *ins* and *outs*, perhaps I had better define this first one quite clearly.

To begin with "*in*," — a low, raftered room with bare floor, three rickety chairs, a bed, and, balanced on the edge of the last-

mentioned article, a bundle of rags sur-
mounted by a mop of tangled hair, to which
it would have puzzled you to give a name,
but which Sandy would have triumphantly
informed you was an unknown quantity
representing his sister Janet, and " *he*
could tell her as far as he could see her."
Is that all ? No ; let me see. There was a
cracked piece of looking-glass, a sulky parrot in a rough wooden cage, and, as I said
before, half of Sandy Dunbar. That is to
say, there was kicking on the floor one
boot and one shoe, with a pair of thin, sun-
burned legs, lost just above the knees in an
old Scotch plaid frock.

" *Out*," you looked down and down, and
saw a narrow street lined on each side with
tall, dingy houses — would you believe it ? —
eight and *nine* stories high ! Every window
was open, and from nearly every one pro-
truded one or more heads, — feeble, white-
haired men, ugly old women with soiled

caps, sickly, pale, tired girls, and kicking, fighting children and babies, that you would almost take for wicked little old men and women. Alas! such bad little faces! If there were any sweetness or innocence left in them, it was buried so deep under layers of dirt that you would quite despair of finding it.

Another thing very curious was that from the upper windows were pushed out wooden frames hung with every imaginable kind of half-washed rags, for these tall stone houses were what is called *tenement* houses, every window representing some one's home; and when washing day came, and they wanted to dry their clothes, all the yard these poor people owned was the yard square of little frame stretching out from their windows.

Down in the street there was no less confusion. Innumerable little stands, covered with gnarled, unwholesome fruit, crowded the.sidewalks. Then there were Jew shops, where old clothes were bought and sold. Faded ball dresses hung out at the doors, dancing and courtesying away as hard as ever; and old bonnets, with dusty, torn flowers, were bobbing politely to rows of battered beavers. Then there was no end of old shirts and coats and dingy shawls, all flapping and waving restlessly in the wind.

Altogether, everything looked so crowded and uncomfortable in this fluttering beggar street, that you could not help having a curious feeling that the dingy houses were filled to overflowing; and from windows and doors, bundles of rags, or of human beings, as it might happen, burst out, as from holes in an enormous over-stuffed rag-bag.

To complete the picture, a carriage was passing through the narrow street with some frightened ladies, who had come from curiosity, but were now afraid to look around them, because of the angry, envious

looks cast upon their pretty dresses. Now
and then some girl with a face full of hate
would make them a mock courtesy, or
malicious boys would make most frightful
grimaces. Indeed, these happy people who
came to take a little look at misery would
not have been at all safe, were it not for
the policemen, who were stationed only a
few steps from each other.

So this was "*out*," with the exception of
a bit of dull sky that was put so far up out
of the way you would never have thought
of noticing it. And, oh! I forgot the other
half of Sandy Dunbar, — the rest of the
plaid frock, a jungle of silky hair, and a
pair of large, restless eyes looking down
into this curious street, the famous " Cow-
gate," in the far-away city of Edinburgh.

To tell you just how Sandy and Janet
came into this dreadful old street would be
a long story, and I know you are all anxious to hear what Sandy saw when he

14

looked out of the window. So I shall only
tell you in a few words that Sandy was
born in America, but when his dear mother
died, about two years ago, his father, who
was a Scotchman, came with his little children back to his native city. At first, they
lived very comfortably; but after a while
the father began to drink, and grew worse
and worse, till at length poverty came upon
them, and chased them from one miserable
home to another, and at last she left them
up eight flights of stairs, in the bare little
attic I have described to you. Here they
led a sad life indeed, for the wretched father didn't do much more than pay the
rent, and often left his little children for
weeks together; so that poor Sandy every
day went working or begging for just enough
to keep alive Janet and himself and old
Jack the parrot, who, I forgot to tell you,
came over the sea with them, and had been
their very dearest friend since their mother

died. There is one more thing I should
tell you, and that is, that poor Janet, coming down the dark, broken stairs, about two
months before, had fallen and sprained her
leg badly, and, as there was no one to help
the forlorn little girl with nice liniments
and bandages, she had suffered very much,
and had been a pining little prisoner ever
since. The days were very long and lonely
while Sandy was away, for Jack would
only be sociable when he pleased, and when
he was hungry would sulk from morning
till night. So poor Janet would drag herself to the window and look out for hours;
and here it was one day that she saw Miri-
am, the little Jew girl, who lived one story
lower down, and was quite aristocratic on
that account, wear a gay little pink ging-
ham apron that Janet thought was the
prettiest one she ever saw in her life. "If
I only had one," thought Janet, "I should
be perfectly happy."

All day long the little girl thought of it, and when Sandy came home, toward night, she told him of it eagerly, with tears in her eyes. " The sweetest apron I ever saw, Sandy ; just the color of a rose."

" You shall have one just like it as soon as I grow to be a man," cried Sandy.

Janet looked grievously disappointed. " I shall be dead before that," she sobbed.

" Oh ! stop that," cried Sandy, in gruff distress as he looked at her thin, white cheeks. Then, catching up her slight figure, he added consolingly to himself, " She's such a mite, and they've got so much to do in that big other world, they'll forget to send for her. Come, Janet," he cried more briskly, " cheer up ! what do you suppose I have got in my pocket ? " and with great triumph he drew out a piece of dry gingerbread and a moldy orange.

Janet gave a little cry of pleasure, and

THE DANCING PARROT.

the parrot twisted his green head and croaked, "Jack wants a cracker."

"I know it," cried Sandy, in an injured tone. "Of course you do; you always do. Didn't I give you half my supper last night? Why can't you be cheerful, and give us one good hurrah?" and Sandy opening the cage door, Jack came scrambling to the floor. "Dance, Jackie," cried Sandy; and Jack lifted gingerly first one claw, then the other, and ended with a great flutter and attempt at a courtesy.

"Good!" cried Sandy, critically. "Now, hurrah! colonel."

"Hurrah!" croaked Jack, in a hoarse, shrill tone, and filled the breast of his little master and mistress with ecstasy.

"There never was such a cunning bird," said Sandy, admiringly. "He could talk just as good as folks, if he was a mind to;" and Janet gave him half the gingerbread.

So these little children for a while forgot all their troubles, and were really merry, till Jack, after some insult to his dignity, retired sulkily to his perch, and would play no more.

Then Janet heaved a long sigh, and remembered the apron.

"Oh, Sandy, I'm *so* lonely all day while you're gone; and if I only had the pretty pink apron, I could play I was queen, and when I got tired I could spread it on the bed, and have nice dreams about sunsets and roses."

Sandy looked troubled. "If I only could earn money, Janet! but nice people won't trust me, because I look like a vagabond; and I get such mean little coppers for running my legs off, that I can't but just keep you and Jack from starving."

"Oh! I knew it was too much," said Janet, with a long sigh; "I knew *I* could never have a pink apron."

The color flushed Sandy's face. Poor,
sick little sister, — the only thing he cared
for in all the world! There was a long
pause, while the gray seemed to fall out of
the sky into the room, and then Sandy
walked irresolutely to the window. He had
scarcely looked out when he caught sight
of the identical pink apron fluttering just
below, and he exclaimed excitedly, "I declare, if she hasn't been washing it, and
hung it right out on the frame!"

"It is the very one," cried Janet, with
devouring eyes. "I can almost touch it
with my hand."

As she spoke, an idea flashed into Sandy's
mind. "Yes," he muttered to himself, "it
isn't far. How careful she's pinned it on,
to be sure, and tied the string round and
round. But I think I can get it. Just
wait till it's darker, and I'll fasten my knife
to a stick, and get astride of the window-
seat, and I think—yes, I'm sure I could

fetch her. Cut the strings on top, give her a pull to the side, and off she'll come, and the little Jew girl will think the wind blew it away. Janet," cried he aloud, "you shall have the pink apron."

"Hurrah, hurrah!" screamed Jack, waking from a doze.

"What can you mean, Sandy?" said Janet, eagerly.

"I'm going to hook it in for you just as soon as it's a little darker, and there comes a row in the streets, so the policemen will be too busy to be looking up."

Janet looked dismayed, and the glow faded from her cheeks. "Don't you remember 'Our Father,' Sandy?" she faltered.

"Oh, the one mother used to tell us about sometimes?" said Sandy, a little dashed; "well, I think I could explain it all to him, how you were sick, and maybe would die if you didn't have the apron, and how the Jew girl had plenty of clothes, and would never miss it, but just have a new one to-morrow."

" But," said Janet, uneasily, " won't thieves have to go to some dreadful place when they die ?"

" Well, now," said Sandy, undauntedly, settling himself upon an old pail, " I'll tell you what I think about it. I don't think 'Our Father,' as you call him, has ever been much of a father to us. We've always had to scratch around the best way we could for ourselves. Now my notion is, that he's a sort of grand policeman, very strong, and with very sharp eyes, and when he sees any one doing anything wrong, he springs on 'em, and shuts 'em up somewhere. But, Janet, *I'm* the greatest fellow to *dodge* you ever saw,—just as slippery as an eel. There isn't an old 'Buttons' on this street that I haven't dodged over and over; and I guess when the right time comes

I can dodge again and slip up to heaven somehow. Then my plan is to hide around for a time, and when they find me at last they won't think it worth while to turn me out."

Janet was lost in admiration of all this wisdom.

"But," added Sandy, "you're a girl, and not up to dodges, and perhaps, to make a safe thing of it, you'd better be good."

An hour afterwards, with great peril, the gay little apron was dragged through the window, and at first Janet laughed with pleasure as she put it on over her rags. But before long she grew very sober.

"Sandy," said she, suddenly, "where is God?"

"Up in the sky somewhere, I've heard," said Sandy, "but I don't know what holds him."

"Can he see in here?"

"Maybe so."

"Well, please pin the quilt up to the window," said she, with her little lips trembling. "Some way I don't want to have him see me with the pink apron on."

It grew darker. The lead had certainly fallen out of the sky into that little room. Janet played "queen" but a very short time, and found no pleasure in it, and then, with a perplexed, disappointed face, she folded the apron carefully and put it under the pillow.

Sandy, too, was ill at ease. "Hurrah, Jackie," cried he, "just once before we go to bed;" but Jack only sunk his head lower in his feathers, and croaked like a feeble old man in pain.

Then they were all very still a long time, —an age it seemed to Sandy,—till he couldn't stand it any longer.

"Janet," he called, "are you asleep?"

"Oh, no," sighed she.

"Well, I feel very queer. I believe I'm sorry I sto— took the pink apron."

CHAPTER II.

A WEEK passed by, and Sandy and Janet had never been so unhappy together.

"Everything seems wrong, some way," said Sandy, coming in one day at noon, and throwing his old cap on the floor.

"I haven't had a decent errand in ever so long. Every one looks cross at me, and calls me thief and beggar, and they might as well say *coward* too, for, Janet, you can't think how queer I'm getting to be. Promise me never to tell."

"Never," said Janet.

"Well, then, really I don't like to be out

220

after dark;" and he laughed an uneasy laugh. "I'm all the time thinking something is behind me, and I jump, and think I must dodge somewhere."

Janet came close to him, looking apprehensively over her shoulder.

"And then I can't think what possesses all the old clothes. They carry on as if they were going into fits, and last night I thought an old policeman was shaking his fist at me, and I dodged. What do you think, Janet? Actually dodged an old coat with one arm most torn out!"

Janet tried to laugh, but it didn't sound very merry, and they were very still a long time, till Jack broke the silence with the most dismal of croaks.

"Oh, Sandy," said Janet, drearily, "I meant to have told you, I think Jack is sick. He sulks all day with his head way down in his neck, and he won't say a word.

If he would only hurrah just once, I know we'd all feel better."

"Jackie, old fellow, I'm afraid you're growing rheumatic;" and Sandy tried to stir him up, but Jack only gave a faint croak, and half closed his filmy eyes. "Maybe he don't get enough to eat, poor fellow! I'd hate to have him die, because he was mother's bird," said Sandy, wiping his eyes. "But what a spoon I'm getting to be. Come now, Jack," said he, breaking into a lively whistle. "Dance your hornpipe, and to-morrow I'll bring you a cracker as big as your head." But Jack's claws seemed glued to his perch.

"It's no use," said Sandy, gloomily. "Everything goes wrong. Why don't you play with your apron, Janet?"

Janet hesitated. "It's too pretty to play with every day," said she at last, but she didn't tell him that it had been laid away three whole days in the little bare closet, and Janet didn't think of roses and sunsets any more when she looked at it.

Sandy looked at her doubtfully a minute; then, muttering something about getting an errand to do, he went heavily out of the room, and heavily, heavily down the stairs. The lodgers he passed on the way looked up with surprise to see only Sandy; they thought it was some one with a heavy load, and if they could have borrowed angels' eyes they would have seen they were not so much mistaken. They would have seen the saddest sight,—a *little* boy carrying a *grown-up* sin.

It was a beautiful day, and Sandy thought he could go over to the lovely gardens that lie between the old and new town, and see the happy people walking there, and perhaps he might pick up some cast-away flowers to bring home to Janet. But on the way Sandy came across something that made him more unhappy still. Before I tell you about it, however, I must first explain that in this good city of Edinburgh you will often see verses from the Bible printed in great big letters, and pasted on the walls and fences wherever the crowd is greatest. So that sometimes, right in the midst of advertisements telling you where to get the best coats and hats, you will read where to buy the " pearl of great price; " or while, before some flaming handbill, you are hesitating whether to go to the concert or theater, you will see close by, — " In God's presence there is *fullness* of joy, — at *his* right hand there are pleasures *for evermore.*" And you can not think how solemn and *real* the words look, printed right out on some great stone page ; very different from where they lie half asleep, as it were, between the red covers of your little Bible. It seems as if they were really meant for *you*, and were sent to you from heaven that very day.

But what happened to Sandy I am going to leave for himself to tell.

It was quite dark when he came clambering back to his little attic, and Janet was sobbing dismally in a corner.

"Oh, Sandy," she exclaimed, "I am afraid Jackie is dead!"

"Well, he's better off than I am then," said Sandy, gloomily, as he looked in the cage where poor Jack, a little heap of rumpled feathers, seemed too feeble for even a croak.

"Don't you know what to do for him?" said Janet, anxiously.

"No, I don't know that, and I'm afraid I don't know anything. I've made a mistake about something I thought I'd got fixed all right. Oh, Janet! I am very unhappy!"

"Why, what is it, Sandy?" cried Janet, forgetting Jackie, in a deeper sympathy.

"Well," began Sandy with an effort, "I'll

15

tell you all about it. When I was crossing over to the new town, I saw something in very big letters on the side of the bridge, and I asked a man what it was. He was laughing at first, but he grew very sober when he read it to me : ' Prepare to meet thy God.' Then I said, ' Please, sir, when is he coming, and does it mean me ? ' But he was in a great hurry, and wouldn't wait to hear me. So I went on, and pretty soon on a wall I saw more big letters, and I did not dare ask what it was, but I heard a woman reading it to her little girl, —' Prepare to meet thy God.'

" Then I began to feel a little frightened, but I went on, and just before I came to the gardens I saw more big letters on a house. I began to know 'em now, but I hoped it was something else, and I was staring away at 'em, when a little boy came along with a beautiful, bright, plaid kilt, and such clean white knees above his pretty stockings. I

knew he was a rich boy and could read, so
I said to him very careless,—'So there is
going to be a show to-night, is there?' and
I pointed to the big words. First he grew
very red, then he said, 'Oh, maybe you can't
read, poor little boy,' and he began very
slow,—'Prepare—' 'Never mind,' I said,
for I couldn't bear to hear it again, 'but
tell me, what does it mean?' 'Mother
would tell you so well,' said he, a little
troubled, 'but I suppose it means that everybody, and you and I, must meet God
when we die, and we must try and be very
good, so we won't be afraid when he sends
for us, but will be all ready to go up and
stand before him in heaven.'

"'Oh, is *that* all?' said I, and I felt a
great deal better, and I told him about my
plan, and how I meant to dodge. But, oh,
Janet, he told me that it was our souls that
went up to God, and souls couldn't dodge.
Besides, God was everywhere, and if they

turned right away from him, and went like
lightning ever so far, when they got there
God would be there before 'em, and it
would be just running into his arms."

" Oh !" said Janet, in a tone of awe.

" Then I said, ' Are you afraid, little boy?'
and he smiled so pleasant.

" ' Oh, no ; mother says God loves little
children, and carries the lambs in his bo-
som.' "

" Oh, how sweet!" said sobbing little Janet.

" But that means *good* children, I suppose," said Sandy, tremulously, "and we —
oh, Janet, God may send for us any time,
for the whole city is full of those dreadful
words ! What *shall* we do ?"

" Try to get ready, Sandy," said Janet,
solemnly.

" Yes, I want to," said Sandy, eagerly,
" but how shall we begin ? I suppose the
first thing is — "

" The *apron*," cried Janet.

" Yes, give it to me this minute, and I'll fasten it on the frame, and the little Jew girl will never know where it has been."

" But one string is cut," said Janet.

Sandy mused. " Janet," cried he at last, in a quivering voice, " it's very hard, but I'll do it. I've earned one penny to-day, and I'll take the penny and the apron, and tell the little Jew girl all about it, and give her the penny to buy a new string."

" But," said Janet, anxiously, " won't she say you're a thief, and have you taken up, and —"

" I can't help it," said Sandy, excitedly. " Some way it seems as if it was right. Suppose God should take me up to-night. Oh, Janet, I'm going to get ready right away. I shall try, oh, how I shall try to be good !"

" And I too," cried Janet.

" Hurrah ! hurrah ! hurrah !" screamed

a shrill voice that brought Sandy and Janet to their feet. There was a great stir in the old wooden cage, and they rushed to the bars. But, alas! it was Jackie's last effort, and he already lay upon his back, with his poor legs growing stiff in the air.

" Well, he hurrahed once more. Dear, *dear* old Jack," said Sandy, the big tears rolling down his cheeks.

Janet kissed the dim feathers. " And I shall always believe," she sobbed, " that he knew it was right to take back the apron."

THE LIGHT UNDER THE DOOR.

THE LIGHT UNDER THE DOOR.

IT can't be that father meant me to clean every bit of this long walk this morning!" pouted Harry Sherman.

"If he only knew how the weeds cling around the bricks, and this old knife slips and cuts me every other minute."

"It's no worse than what I've got to do," cried Fret number two, in the person of Susy Sherman. "Here's this monstrous pan of peas to shell, and I don't know but it will take me the rest of my life. There, Fifine," said she, flinging her big doll in a corner. "You're always smirking and smiling, no matter what trouble I'm in. Now you may go to bed till dinner-time. Oh dear! what horrid times we do have!"

"Don't you wish," cried Harry, as Susy settled herself disconsolately on the back stoop, "that we could wake up some morning in a palace, and find that we were princes?"

"Princesses, you mean," said Susy, amending the word to suit her stand-point. "Yes, indeed! I should not get up till ten o'clock, and then I wouldn't even put on my stockings. Two or three maids, at least, should dress me in gold lace and diamonds, and braid flowers in my hair, and—"

"Pshaw!" interrupted Harry. "Girls always think of dress the first thing. Now *I* should first take my breakfast,—chicken, soup, ice-cream, buckwheat cakes, and pie, and nuts!"

"And boys," retorted Susy, "are always thinking of something to eat."

" Wait a minute till I finish," cried Harry.
" Then I should have a *Duke* — nothing
less — knock very respectfully at the door,
and say, ' Will your highness please ride
on your Arab pony? Or would you like to
review the troops, and see them all go bare-
headed the moment you come in sight,
while the band plays ' God save the King ' ?
Or would you like to lie on the divan in
the court by the fountain, and have a hundred birds with red and blue feathers,
singing sweeter than nightingales? And
shall I bring your majesty the ' Arabian
Nights,' with a thousand pictures colored in
oil, or Robinson Crusoe, with a million
pictures? Then I'd choose one, and give
him a sort of terrible look, and he'd fly to
get it. Then one slave should fan me, and
another turn over my leaves, and I wouldn't
hear any one saying a dozen times a day,
' Harry, isn't that a little selfish ? ' or,
' Harry, I'd be ashamed to be so lazy ! '

No, indeed; it would all be 'your majesty!' 'your highness!' Then they'd bow till their heads bumped the floor, and whatever I did, they'd say, 'How princely!' 'How graceful!' 'How condescending!' Oh! it would be great to be a prince!"

Susy, absently twisting a pea-pod, gave a long sigh of acquiescence. Why she had been chosen to open her eyes in an old red farm-house instead of a palace, was a piece of injustice she couldn't at all understand.

"Good-morning, little ones," said a kindly voice, breaking in suddenly upon these meditations.

"Oh! Mr. Benson," cried Susy, a little confused, as their old gray-haired pastor moved slowly up the walk. "How long have you been here?"

"Not a great while, child," he said, smiling; "but I am going to stay long enough to tell you and Harry a little story while you are at work."

The faces brightened, and he began : —

" Far across the sea, in the grand palace of the Louvre, hangs a picture so sweet and so sad, I do not think you, Harry or Sue, could look at it five minutes without your little hearts trembling up into a great sob.

" Now listen to every word I say, and perhaps I can manage to hang it up before your eyes. First, you see a room very dim, with great black shadows hiding in the heavy beams overhead. The narrow windows are like slits in the thick wall, and the small panes are quite black now, for it is night,—in fact, very near midnight. Still, you can see a bed and two little children sitting upon it, for a little light streams in under the heavy door, — a dull red light; — what can it be ? "

" The little children are frightened," suggested Sue, " and their mother or Aunt Jenny is coming with a candle, to kiss them and cover them up."

" Alas, no, poor innocents!" said Mr.
Benson. " Let us look at them a little
more closely. They are two boys, whom
the artist has dressed very handsomely,
though I do not know that it is in gold lace."
Susy blushed again. " Their faces are very
noble and sweet, and the younger boy's
cheeks are rosy and full, while the elder
one is sickly and pale as a lily, and lays his
poor, tired head on his brother's strong
young shoulder. In his slender hand, so
small under the broad ruffles at the wrist,
the sick boy holds a book, — a little prayer-
book, which they probably were reading the
last thing before the room grew so dark.
They didn't seem to have had any slave to
turn the book, however, although they were
princes, — royal princes, and born in a palace. No, they were all alone, with the exception of a faithful little dog, who stood
on the floor, with his ears pricked up, listening, listening to some noise; some foot,

perhaps, coming softly. What do you suppose he heard?"

"It was a duke or a lord, I suppose," said Harry, "coming to tell them that their father, the king, was willing they should get up to the court ball, or to see some grand torchlight procession, or something."

"But their father, the king, was dead; had died very lately."

"Oh!" returned Harry, briskly. "Then I suppose they were coming to tell that sick young prince that *he* was king, and to ask him if he would please be crowned to-morrow."

"Not with any earthly crown, poor boy!" said Mr. Benson. "This poor prince should indeed have been king; he *was* the rightful King of England,—great, rich England; but he had a wicked uncle, deformed and humpbacked, who was determined to have the throne for himself. This cruel uncle was very deceitful. He pretended to the little princes that he was their very best friend, while all the time he was killing all the good, honorable men who would have protected them.   Then, with many fair words, he took them away from their poor mother, and persuaded them to go into a strong old fortress, called the Tower.   Little did they think when they passed through those gloomy gates that they would never come out in the sunshine again, poor babies."

"Why, he didn't hurt the pretty princes, did he?" cried Sue.   "Why didn't somebody stop him?"

"Nobody dared, for he had made himself king, and was very powerful.   There was only one thing he feared, and that was that some day the little princes would get out of the Tower, and the people would say, 'There's the true king!   Let us kill the Humpback!'

"So he made up his mind that they must die, and he hired some cruel men to go at midnight and kill the little Prince of Wales and Duke of York in their beds."

"Do such things truly ever happen to princes?" said Harry, incredulously.

"Indeed they do! Kings and princes have often been the most unhappy and unfortunate men in the world,—have been imprisoned, tortured, beheaded,—have died most violent and terrible deaths. Have you never heard the saying, 'Uneasy lies the head that wears a crown'? That is too true. The higher one is in life the more there are to envy him, and want to pull him down."

Harry gave a low whistle. He had never thought of that. It was some comfort that no one would care to kill *him* to fall heir to his old knife and weed-digging.

"But," interposed Susy, "did the murderers really get in and kill the sweet young princes?"

"Yes," said Mr. Benson, thoughtfully;

16

"they were smothered in bed with their own pillows. It is all over now," said he, wiping away a tear; "the fluttering little hearts have been at rest many, many years; but I can never forget that picture, and the terrible moment it represented. Think of it again, dear children, — the gloomy room; the dog listening so eagerly, bristling with anger and terror; the little princes, with sweet, frightened faces, clasped in each other's arms, watching that strange light. They did not know who was bringing it; they could not have imagined what evil was coming upon them; but the cruel red light kept creeping, creeping under the door, and they watched, wondering, one dreadful moment, while outside the murderers were coming softly, stealthily, nearer, *nearer !* "

"Don't tell any more, please," cried Susy, dropping her peas, and sobbing under her apron.

"Well, to be sure. I did not want to

trouble the little heart. But just one word more," said Mr. Benson, smiling. "How do you suppose the little princes would have felt, now, if, when the door opened, there had only come a messenger to say, 'The Prince of Wales must weed the garden-walk for an hour, and the Duke of York must shell a pan of peas'?"

Susy laughed hysterically, and Harry hung his head.

"They wouldn't have thought it very '*horrid*,' would they? Wouldn't they have danced and wept for joy? I wonder how often the poor princes, in their solemn old Tower, torn away from their dear mother, would have envied the happy boys born in little red farm-houses, quiet and safe, running in the blessed sunshine, with no one to grudge them their poor little lives."

"All princes are not smothered in their beds, though," said Harry, half to himself.

"No," said Mr. Benson, overhearing

him ; " but they all have their troubles soon or late, just as surely as the little farmers. There is no escape. Let us learn, dear children, in whatsoever state we are, therewith to be content."

CINDER ELLA.

245

CINDER ELLA.

HERE, I thought you'd cry," said Regan, angrily. "How unreasonable you are! I've told you a dozen times that you were only asked out of politeness, and there won't be another such little snip as *you* are there. Nobody will want to play with you, and you will just be in everybody's way."

"But I want to go," sobbed Ella.

"Of course you do," said Babette. "You always want to do everything that is selfish and contrary."

"But I won't ask anybody to play with me," pleaded Ella, "and I won't be in the way. I'll just look on and keep as still as a mouse."

" But you're such a fright," persisted Regan. " Your face is brown as a berry, and such black hands! I don't suppose they'd come clean if you soaked them all night. How do you suppose I'll feel if I have to tell any one you're my sister? Why, you'll look like a toad at a butterfly's ball ! "

Ella's eyes grew large with horror. " Do I look so very bad ? " quivered she.

" A dirty little thing ! " cried Babette, emphatically. " You look as if you were dug out of an ash-heap, — black as a cinder ! "

" Ha ! " laughed Regan ; " that's a good idea. ' Black as a cinder ! ' Let's call her Cinder Ella ! "

" Well, you know why I'm dirty now, sobbed Ella. " You know you said this morning that if I'd only weed all the beds,

you wouldn't say a word against my going.
Just think if I had left yours how father
would have scolded when he got home. It
was *such* hard work too in the sun! " said
Ella, bursting into fresh tears, " and now
it's all for nothing! "

" Dear me! what a plague! " cried Regan,
uneasily. "I suppose we'll have to let you
go. But, Cinder Ella, you must help *us*
first."

" Oh yes," cried little Ella, joyfully, dry-
ing her tears. " I'll do anything in the
world."

" Curl my hair first," cried Regan.

" And then braid mine," said Babette.

" And lace up my shoes," said Regan.
" It tires me so to stoop over. And then
fasten my dress, and — "

" And then you will show me how to
mend that hole in my white dress, won't
you? and how I must baste the lace in the
neck," said Ella, coaxingly.

"Not I, goose!" said Regan, rolling her great eyes scornfully. "I've no time for that!"

"Nor I," said Babette.

"It wouldn't take long," pleaded Ella.

"A day's work at least," snapped Regan; "I shan't take the first stitch."

"But what *will* I do then?" said Ella, beginning to choke.

"Oh, no one will look at *you*, Cinder; you can wear your white dimity."

"Why, that's almost a baby dress, and so small—so small—with a string around the neck just like a baby. What *shall* I do?"

"Well, you're a dreadful trial!" said Regan, with a long sigh. "You're never satisfied. I'm tired of hearing such fretting. Come, Babette, let's go."

"What, without *me?*" cried Cinder Ella. "Isn't any one going to help *me?*"

"Oh, you're too cross and ill-tempered," cried Regan; "and besides, it's getting very late. You know the way well enough, and can come when you get ready."

Cinder Ella saw them go, with streaming eyes. "Pray, Mrs. Beaver," cried she, meeting the housekeeper as she turned back into the hall, "will you help me dress?"

"Not I, Moppet," said she, briskly. "I've got a dozen other irons in the fire;" and she bustled away into the pantry.

"Oh, if *mother* was only alive!" sobbed Cinder Ella as she again turned away.

"How now?" cried a loud, clear voice, that made Ella jump as if a bugle had sounded in her ear. "I declare, if it isn't all in a Scotch mist! I can hardly tell whether it's a girl or a rose-bush!"

"Oh, dear, dear Miss Cherie!" cried Ella, throwing herself into the arms of the queerest dried-up little lady, — homelier than any old fairy in her hundred and first year, — "I *must* tell you all about it;" and then Cinder Ella's tongue beat the dismalest kind of a tattoo upon the drum of Miss Cherie's ear for about ten minutes, at the end of which time that kind old lady cried,—

"Well, my little Cinder Ella, I'll be your fairy godmother. I remember how these little feet came every day to run my errands when I had the rheumatism last winter, and now they shall run for their own pleasure, if I can help them."

So the soft golden hair was brushed into shining curls, and the plain dimity was beautified with a rose ribbon around the waist, and some wild flowers, which Cinder Ella had found in the woods, were twined in a lovely wreath around her head.

"There, darling," said Miss Cherie, kissing her; "I'm sorry I haven't some mice and a pumpkin shell, but I guess your own little feet will do as well;" and Cinder Ella, all smiles and dimples, set out for the party. It was almost sunset when she came in sight of the house, and saw the garden, with its trees, and fountains, and flowers, and the happy children flitting in and out through the shaded walks. Supper was just ready in the arbor, and as she reached it, Victor Talbot—the young master of the feast—came ushering in his guests, leading the pretty Regan by the hand.

"Who is this?" he cried, as his eye fell upon the little girl standing on tiptoe at the end of the arbor, her innocent face glowing with delighted surprise. "See her cheeks and her hair, all crimson and gold; she must have dropped out of the sunset!"

"It is Cinder," said Regan, in an angry whisper to Babette, who was just behind.

"Anything but a cinder *now*," retorted Babette in a tone of still greater vexation.

" Sly little minx ! What can she have done to make herself look so pretty ? "

" It must be the baby waist that is so becoming. Who would have thought it ? " said Regan.

" No, I'm sure it's the wreath," cried Babette. But neither of them was right.

All this was done in a minute, and then Regan turned very amiably to Victor, and said, —

" That is our *sister.*"

" Oh, said Victor, " I am very glad she has come ;" and taking her by the hand, he brought her to the head seat at the table, and gave her the prettiest bon-bons he could find.

" How kind every one is to me," whispered the delighted Cinder Ella to her sister.

Regan gave her an angry look, and just whispered, " Sly little rat ! "

" Why, what is the matter ? " asked Cinder Ella, piteously, opening her big blue eyes. "My hands are very clean. Are you ashamed of me? Did I get in anybody's way?" But Regan only tossed her head.

"Where did you get those pretty flowers?" asked Babette.

"In the woods this morning.

"Are there any more? Will you show me where?"

"Oh yes!" said Cinder Ella, delighted to do anything to oblige. "But we'll have to hurry, it will be dark so soon."

"I'll go too," said Regan; and the two sisters could hardly wait till supper was over to drag Cinder Ella away into the woods.

They soon found the flowers, and forgiving Cinder Ella, who had the most taste, was busily making them into wreaths, when they heard a groan a little way off. Regan, who was a great coward, turned white as her handkerchief. "Let's run!" cried she. "Never mind the wreaths." But Cinder Ella parted the bushes, and there, upon the ground, lay foolish little Robin Campbell, with his big mouth all puckered in with pain.

"What is the matter, Robin?" said Cinder Ella, kindly.

"Fall!" cried Robin, his mouth expanding big as a coffee-cup, with a great cry. "Broke!" he continued, piteously, pointing to one limp foot.

"Don't bother with the goose," cried Regan. "Finish our wreaths, and let's hurry back to the party. We're losing beautiful games, I know."

"He's afraid," cried Robin. "Take him home."

"Walk home yourself, you little plague!" cried Babette; "there's nothing the matter with you;" and she lifted him rudely to his feet; but poor Robin fell down again with a piteous cry.

"Let's try to carry him home," said Cinder Ella; "it's only a little way."

"Not I, indeed," cried Regan; "I should soil my dress."

"And I should make my hands dirty and red," said Babette.

"I'll go and call your mother, poor Robin," said Cinder Ella, "and *she* will carry you home."

"No! no!" shrieked Robin. "Don't leave him; he's afraid. The dark makes faces at him!"

Cinder Ella looked imploringly at her sisters.

"You needn't say a word," cried Regan, gathering up her flowers. "If you *must* be so silly as to prefer staying with this half-witted Robin, you can't expect us to keep you company. We'll finish our wreaths ourselves, and go back to the party. We've lost a great deal of time already;" and the two sisters turned down a foot-path, and were soon lost to sight.

Poor Cinder Ella was in great perplexity. She couldn't stay there all night, and if she ran for help Robin would go into a fit with fright, and perhaps die. She must just try to carry him herself, for he was a little smaller than she, and sickly besides, poor fellow! and couldn't be very heavy. So she tenderly lifted the sobbing boy, and staggered off through the woods. The way was longer than she thought, and Robin grew heavier every moment. She found herself in a terribly muddy place once, and when she at last got out one little foot had lost its slipper. But the brave heart never lost its courage, and at last, all panting, with torn dress, and ready to cry with fatigue, she put little Robin safe in his mother's arms, and heard the poor woman bless her and thank her a thousand times for befriending the poor Robin, "who hadn't the wit of a gosling, and might have died with pain and fright before his mother could have found him."

Poor Cinder Ella was in no plight to go back to the party, and she stole quietly through the by-paths.

Mrs. Beaver scolded well when she saw her. "Dirty little thing! Had she been with the pigs? No wonder they called her *'Cinder* Ella.' Her two sisters would come home looking as if they had just stepped out of a bandbox, but as for her little dimity — " Mrs. Beaver held up her hands in horror, though I don't believe the angels saw a spot on it.

The next day, as the sisters sat in the porch, Regan suddenly exclaimed, "Oh! here comes Victor Talbot, and Philo, and Max, and two or three others. Run, Cinder Ella, and get my blue ribbons and my silk apron."

" And my scarlet net, and a clean hand-kerchief," cried Babette, "and then run away to your own room, and stay till they are gone. Of course they don't want to see *you*."

The orders were all obeyed, and the blue ribbons and red net just settled in place as Victor came up.

"Good-morning," he cried. "I haven't a minute to lose. We intend having a festival of roses while this fine weather lasts, and we think it would be pleasant to have a king and queen of the flowers. I have been chosen king, and have come to select my queen."

Regan rolled her eyes, which were very large and handsome, and Babette smiled to show her teeth, which were white and regular as pearls.

"Just now, as we came through the woods," continued Victor, abruptly, "I met my old nurse, and she had a long story

to tell me of some kind little girl who had
carried her poor simple Robin home, when
he had hurt his foot, and was almost dying
with pain and fright alone in the woods.
She said the dear little girl must have had
a great struggle to carry him so far, and
she feared she had lost one of her shoes,
for she had just found one in the swamp
hard by. So we boys, who had just been
talking about our queen, made up our
minds that the girl who could do such a
kind act must be beautiful enough, whoever she might be, to be queen of the
flowers. Here is the shoe that held the
kind little foot," said he, holding up a
muddy little slipper, "and I've come like
the prince in the fairy tale. Whoever can
wear it shall be my queen! Is it *yours*,
Regan?"

Regan blushed. "I can wear it," she
said, "but my foot is swollen this morning."

Babette gave her an angry look. "You know you can hardly get it on your great toe," she said in a loud whisper.

"You were the kind girl, then, Babette," said Victor. "Let me fit it on your foot."

"Yes," said Babette, "I did lift the little boy, I remember."

"Oh, Babette!" began Regan, but Babette interrupted with a little scream, as the shoe pinched her cruelly.

"The shoe is on the wrong foot," cried Philo, who never did like Regan and Babette. "Call Ella, — pretty Cinder Ella!"

Regan and Babette made no haste to go, but Philo waylaid Mrs. Beaver, and blushing little Ella soon made her appearance.

"How is this?" cried Max, looking down at her feet, just peeping from her dress; "one slipper and one gaiter! Where's the mate to this slipper?"

Cinder Ella blushed still more.

" Here ! " said Victor, and kneeling down he tried it on, when the foot and slipper sprang together like old acquaintances, as indeed they were.

" Here is the queen of the flowers ! " cried Victor, kissing the brown hand.

" Hurrah ! " cried the boys. " Three times three for Queen Cinder Ella ! " And Mrs. Beaver told Miss Cherie that Regan and Babette ran away to the garret and " cried their eyes *out*," though this might have been an exaggeration.

CLARIBEL'S PRAYERS.

265

CLARIBEL'S PRAYERS.

THE day, with cold, gray feet, clung shivering
    to the hills,
While o'er the valley still night's rain-fringed
    curtains fell;
But waking Blue Eyes smiled, "'Tis ever as
    God wills;
He knoweth best, and be it rain or shine, 'tis
    well.
Praise God!" cried always little Claribel.

Then sank she on her knees. With eager,
    lifted hands,
Her rosy lips made haste some dear request
    to tell:
"Oh, Father! smile, and save this fairest of all
    lands,
And make her free, whatever hearts rebel.
Amen! Praise God!" cried little Claribel.

"And, Father," still arose another pleading
   prayer,
  "Oh save my brother, in the rain of shot
    and shell;
Let not the death-bolt, with its horrid, stream-
   ing hair,
  Dash light from those sweet eyes I love so
    well.
  Amen! Praise God!" wept little Claribel.

"But, Father, grant that when the glorious fight
   is done,
  And up the crimson sky the shouts of free-
    men swell, —
Grant that there be no nobler victor 'neath the
   sun
  Than he whose golden hair I love so well.
  Amen! Praise God!" cried little Claribel.

When gray and dreary day shook hands with
   grayer night,
  The heavy air was thrilled with clangor of a
    bell.

" Oh, shout!" the herald cried, his worn eyes
 brimmed with light;
 " 'Tis victory! Oh what glorious news to
  tell!"
 " Praise God! He heard my prayer," cried
 Claribel.

" But pray you, soldier, was my brother in the
 fight,
 And in the fiery rain? Oh! fought he brave
  and well?"
" Dear child," the herald cried, "there was no
 braver sight
 Than his young form, so grand 'mid shot and
  shell."
 " Praise God!" cried trembling little Claribel.

" And rides he now with victor's plumes of red,
 While trumpets' golden throats his coming
  steps foretell?"
The herald dropped a tear. " Dear child," he
 softly said,
 " Thy brother evermore with conquerors
  shall dwell."

" Praise God! He heard my prayer," cried
Claribel.

" With victors, wearing crowns and bearing
palms," he said,
And snow of sudden fear upon the rose lips
fell.
" Oh! sweetest herald, say my brother lives,"
she plead.
" Dear child, he walks with angels, who in
strength excel:
Praise God, who gave this glory, Claribel."

The cold, gray day died sobbing on the weary
hills,
While bitter mourning on the night wind
rose and fell.
" Oh, child," the herald wept, " 'tis as the dear
Lord wills;
He knoweth best, and, be it life or death, 'tis
well."
" Amen! Praise God!" sobbed little Clari-
bel.